PRAXIS II

PRAXIS MAKES PERMANENT

PRAXIS II

PRAXIS MAKES PERMANENT

DAVID GERROLD

STAR TRAVELER PRESS

ISBN-13: 979-8-9930162-2-1

Praxis II: Praxis Makes Permanent copyright © 2025 by David Gerrold

Editor and Publisher: Justin T. O'Conor Sloane

Cover art: *Jim Discovers Saturn* © 2025 by Bob Eggleton

Book design by Katerina Bruno

Star Traveler Press
an imprint of Starship Sloane Publishing Company, Inc.
Austin-Round Rock Metro, Texas, USA
starshipsloane.com

CONTENTS

ONE

T he train was impressive on the outside—
a chain of huge pill-shaped cars, each one
as wide as five ordinary train cars. They
had to be wide to hold all the supplies and the
massive equipment the colony would need—and
the cars needed to be large because there was a
limit on how long a train could be, so each car
needed to be its own self-sufficient environment,
as the whole train was going to pass through
multiple hostile environments, low-gravity, high-
gravity, low-pressure, high pressure, possible
storms, probable vacuum, and a few below-ground
tunnels so the contents—us—wouldn't get roasted
by heat or radiation.

It was impressive on the inside too. The cars
had an airlock at each end, and connecting airlocks
between them. Depending on the cargo, each car
could have five distinct floors, although some did
not, just a large open space for bulky cargo and
heavy equipment.

When a car did have floors, the bottom

level was all the machinery and supplies for maintaining a livable environment, air and water especially. The next floor up was storage and cargo. Above that were cabins, lounge, galley and service areas and additional survival equipment. If necessary, every level could be pressurized and sealed. But it wasn't cramped. It felt like a luxury cruise ship. I'd only seen pictures, so maybe I was imagining, but I could see why the trains had to be comfortable. We'd be living here for quite a while. Some trains had taken two months to reach their destinations. Even farther out, possibly longer.

José and I found our cabin easily. We closed the door behind us, looked at each other, and after a long uncertain moment, we hugged. And after a longer moment, we even started laughing. "We've come a long way."

"And we still have a long way to go."

I pulled down the bed so we could sit side by side. I put my arm around his shoulders and pulled him close. I looked at us in the mirror opposite, met his gaze and said, "Thank you."

"For . . . ?"

"For everything."

"Uh-huh, yes," he agreed. "Everything."

Well, not everything. We still had a lot to talk about, but we'd have time.

Our journey to Praxis was expected to take two weeks, maybe three, or maybe even as long as a month, depending on the amount of traffic up and down the line.

Most people don't understand how the portals work, even the intelligence engines aren't certain. They just juggle the probabilities and most of the time they get it right. Most of the time.

A portal is a hole in space. It opens to another . . . place. There are two ways to make a portal. One is to open a zero-based portal, go through it, grab the other side and schlep it off to someplace useful. So if you were to open a portal in New York, grab the other side of it and drag it off to London, you would have a big circular doorway direct from Times Square to Piccadilly Circus, which is great for shopping, exchange rates, and the rapid spread of viral mutations.

Or you could grab that other side, and launch it off to Luna or Mars. The result is a known portal that lets a person travel off-planet for the cost of a ticket—but tourism to Luna or Mars isn't cheap, what drains your wallet is the cost of survival once you get there.

But it's still cheaper than the whole space travel adventure, which I am told can get pretty boring for passengers after the second or third day. It's not like a cruise ship. It's cramped, high-gee acceleration is uncomfortable, the internal machinery of the ship is loud, and if the idea of using everyone's recycled water for drinking (or what passes for bathing in free fall) gives you the squicks, then travel by portal is a much easier alternative. In short, space travel still belongs to engineers and billionaires who like to be dramatic.

The important thing about portals is that they provide cost-effective access. You can load up a cargo pod with all your supplies, all your survival necessities, and all your heavy machinery, and go. You find a nice stable place, you can build the strongest containment possible, a really strong containment where you don't have to worry about maybe blowing a Montana-sized crater in the landscape and once you're off Earth, you can safely generate multiple portals and launch them all over the solar system. When those distant doorways are all in place and functioning, you have portals direct to Ganymede, Titan, Europa, Ceres, parts of Mercury, Sedna, and anywhere else anyone is willing to pay for.

Putting portals all over the solar system is a great time-saver for scientists, astronomers, and industrialists who want to dig mines for stuff without having to worry about environmental protections. Once the first few billions are recovered, portals can be cost-effective. There's a lot of tourist travel too, but most off-planet resorts are still sealed environments.

Sending a portal to another star system is a whole other problem, because you have to send the other side of the hole to the desired destination before you can step through.

It requires a starship.

TWO

I t's not impossible.
 Because the portal is already open and you can pump fuel directly through the portal to keep the outbound ship under constant acceleration.

And if the ship is unmanned, it can accelerate more than one-gee. You can build up some pretty good vee, almost 1/5 C, a fifth of the speed of light. But it's expensive, hard to get through various budget committees. There's a portal aimed at Proxima Centauri and another one at Sirius, I think, and there's some talk about exploring other nearby stars. But there are too many cheaper opportunities, a lot more cost-effective.

It's the other way to use a portal.

You can open a portal to nowhere.

First you run the numbers, a lot of numbers, sometimes enough numbers to compute the circumference of the universe down to the last nanometer. The computations use a lot of processing, and then quite a bit more to build the necessary equipment, power it up and test it extensively, but when confidence is finally high enough, you turn on the quantum defibrillator and punch a hole in space.

If it opens up to someplace really dangerous, like the inside of a planet or a star or a black hole, which shouldn't happen, but there's a lot of stuff that happens that shouldn't happen, so if the portal detects an impossible energy balance, the system shuts down without ever opening, and you wipe your forehead and say, "Well, it seemed like a good idea at the time."

Otherwise, if the portal detects a workable balance, you send in a probe. It looks around and reports back. If you don't like what you see, you shut it down and redo your numbers. If it seems even marginally useful, you go through, take a better look around, and if you think this place might be profitable, or even useful as an outbound transit station, you secure the portal in place and lay tracks.

Wherever it is, you now have a doorway to somewhere.

The problem is, you won't know where that somewhere is.

Because wherever that portal is, you'll never know what galaxy you've arrived at.

You can study the sky forever, looking for landmarks like known pulsars, but so far nobody has identified any place where any of those far off portal destinations might be located. And a lot of people have looked. At last count, there were over at least three trillion galaxies in the universe, probably a lot more. I'm not a cosmologist, I just know it's a lot more than a lot.

One more thing.

All exploratory portals are opened off-planet, usually on some intermediate transit rock. It's done this way because there's a hole in Montana large enough to drop a mountain in. Several mountains. Really big mountains. No, bigger than that. After the dust settled, everybody who was in a position to have an opinion decided that all outbound portals should be opened off-planet. As far away as possible.

Blow-outs don't happen often, but often enough that a career as a portal engineer is not for people who read trilogies.

But that's why all the transit stations are triple-contained and triple-airlocked—on both sides. There are people, intelligent people, who fear that might not be enough, but there we are. The assumption is that if there's ever another blowout, the containment dome will provide enough time to collapse the hole before the rest of the landscape gets sucked off into some unknown black hole.

This has never been tested. It might be enough, but who knows?

Outbound portals always open to transition stations—usually barren worlds like Mars or airless rocks like Luna—and from there, other portals open to habitable worlds or more often, worlds where mineral resources can profitably be mined. Portals have to be kept apart from each other, something about stress field interference, which meant that portal trains usually have to travel a bunch of kilometers from the inbound portal to the outbound. Portals have to match complex equations of possibilities for both sides of the hole, so sometimes inbound and outbound holes have to be hundreds of kilometers apart, so wherever anyone wants to go, whether it's an industrial station or a settled colony, it's going to require a lot of travel from one portal to the next, from one world to the next.

The route map is like a tree with branches spreading outward from a single seed. Or maybe it's like a dandelion, with multiple branches exploding outward from multiple branches from a single stem. Choose your own analogy.

To get from one world to another means going up or down the branches until you find a common branch that reaches them both. But then, whether or not you can get there depends on if the route is available from your station to the other one. The lower down the tree you have to go, the harder it is to secure track time. Some rocks host as many as a dozen outbound portals. And because there are more trains than available connections or tracks, routing between the portals can get difficult. A single missed connection can screw up schedules as far out as Athena.

There, that's everything you need to know about portals.

Unless you're traveling. Then it's a whole other experience.

THREE

For those who are emigrating, Luna and Mars are just stopovers—those portals open to transit stations, uninhabited rocks hosting other outbound portals.

For emigrants, like José and myself, the journey to Praxis is one-way only. Outbound.

Because Praxis, like a few other habitable worlds, has native life of its own—mostly primitive. Maybe safe, maybe not. No one is sure. So no one is taking chances. Nothing from out there and nothing exposed to anything out there was ever going to be allowed to come back here.

We were bused to someplace in South Dakota, blurred out on the maps, where we boarded the train, thirty to a car. After we found our cabins, we met in the lounge and sat through a recorded orientation, telling us what we could do for the duration of the journey, what we couldn't do, and what we absolutely shouldn't even think about doing. Then we were dismissed back to our cabins and told to get some rest, we wouldn't be moving out until final checks were completed.

Our cabin wasn't large, but it wasn't cramped either. One wall was a screen that could reveal the outside view, or any other display we might want. There was a large fold-out bed, a closet, drawers, a desk, a chair, a sofa, and if we pulled rolled back the floorboards, there was a treadmill wide enough for two. There was a community shower, lav, and gym at the end of the corridor and we were encouraged to keep ourselves clean and fit. Just because we weren't in the training room didn't mean our training was over.

José and I sat on the bed and held hands and caught our breath. Despite all the waiting, it still felt like it was happening too fast.

Finally, I turned to him and said, "Well, here we are."

"Uh-huh."

"Any regrets?"

"I think it's a little late for that."

"No, we could still quit. They said that in the orientation."

He shook his head and smiled. "Do you want to?"

"Nuh-uh."

"I didn't think so."

I reached over and took his hand. We sat quiet for a moment. "So . . ."

"So . . . ?"

"I was thinking."

11

"Uh-oh."

"No, it was good thinking."

"Okay."

"I mean . . . we're married, right?"

"Uh-huh."

"So . . ." I stopped. I wasn't sure how to say it. I just knew it had to be said. "Um—"

He waited.

"I know you're you . . . and I'm me."

"Uh-huh."

"And I'm not asking you to change. I mean, I think we're doing pretty good, so far . . ."

"Uh-huh. Yeah." He nodded thoughtfully. "So . . ."

"Well, um, I was thinking that maybe, if sometime, maybe you think you might want to change, you know, then I would be willing to change with you. I mean, if that's something you might want."

José squeezed my hand. "Thank you," he said. And then he added, "*Si, mi amor.*"

"So, um?"

"Well . . ." He rubbed his face, something he did when he was thinking hard. "It's not something we have to decide tonight. We should wait and see how things work out, okay?"

"Uh-huh. Yes. I just wanted to let you know that . . . well, we've been through a lot and you've been there for me when I needed you and—"

"You've been there for me too—"

"So . . ."

"*Si*," he said. "*Comprendo*."

We sat quietly for a little while, maybe a long while, then abruptly he turned and hugged me. Tight. And I hugged him back. Just as tight. And then he kissed me. Because sometimes that's what husbands do. Because they're husbands.

FOUR

After a bit, José said, "Let's get some coffee." We found our way to the galley for a late-night snack, coffee and sandwiches, not too bad. We joined Alec, Hunter, and Tyler at a table, and the five of us just looked at each other and grinned. There wasn't really much to say. Mostly small talk.

"How's your cabin?"

"Same as yours."

Alec was studying something on his tablet. José nudged him gently.

"Everything okay?"

Alec nodded. "Mostly."

"Huh?"

"We left in a hurry. We never got to the last part of the training. We'll have to make it up on the way."

Tyler grinned. "It never ends."

I said, "That's not news."

Alec looked across the table at both of us. "You know what we kept saying in the training room? 'The easy part is over.' That's true over and over, again and again, every time you get out of bed. For the rest of your lives."

"Yeah, so? That's what we signed up for. You told us at the beginning it's going to be an adventure."

He smiled. "Do you know what the definition is of an adventure?"

José said, "Something exciting?"

Alec shook his head. "That's just the emotion. No. An adventure is any situation where something is at risk. Your integrity, your identity, your life."

José didn't answer immediately. Neither did I. Finally, I said, "It's still better than the alternative. This way . . . well, we're not slaves anymore, are we?"

Alec leaned back in his chair. "Okay, that's a good answer. But it's not enough. What's your definition of freedom?"

"I think it's what you said in the training room. It's being responsible for our own choices. Well—" I gestured around the lounge. "Here we are. This is what we chose." And I poked José next to me. "And this is who I choose to do it with." José poked me. Hard. I said, "Well, he chose me first. And, uh—to tell the truth, I've even kinda sorta fallen in love with him. I mean, you know, in a buddy kind of way."

"Just a buddy kind of way?" asked Tyler, with a slight grin.

"Well, um . . . for the moment, yeah. We've only been married for three months, three and a half. Give us a chance."

Their laughter was interrupted by a chime. Alec glanced to his tablet. "That was the five-minute warning. We're about to move. You might want to strap in. The first portal goes to Luna. It might be a shock."

"You've done this before?"

Alec nodded. "Sometimes, some of the trainers ride along. To function as hosts. To keep you from slacking off. And to continue any last parts of the training. We try to do as much as we can to prepare you before we turn you loose. Once you guys go out the airlock, you're there. Those of us who plan on coming back, we don't get exposed to Praxis."

"So you could still return?"

"I could. Yes." He paused. "But not this time. There's this about trainings. Trainers are always getting trained too." He scratched his cheek thoughtfully. " I've had enough training. I'm going."

"Do other trainers emigrate?"

"Some of them. Not all. It's usually the ones who don't have families."

José spoke up then. "So . . . what you're saying, anyone else could still come back? Right up to the last moment?"

Alec nodded. "We don't say much about it, but yeah, you still have one last chance to opt out . . ."

But there was something he wasn't saying.

José's eyes narrowed. "Or . . . what?"

Alec spoke slowly. "Well, I guess I can tell you. It doesn't happen often, but the colony reviews every application when we arrive. It's mostly a formality, but . . . sometimes an immigrant gets sent back."

"Rejected?"

Alec nodded again.

There was silence for a moment.

"How often does that happen?"

"Not much anymore. The trainings are designed to produce results. We're always adjusting the processes. We try to drop the obvious ones early. As you saw."

José cleared his throat. "You played some serious tricks on us."

"We ran specific exercises, yes. They worked, didn't they?"

José nodded, but he didn't smile.

"You feel manipulated, don't you?"

José half-nodded.

Alec reached over and touched his hand. "You're not the first. It's a normal reaction." He added, "I'll tell you something else. That feeling? It's useful. It's one of the root emotions of empathy. Practice that and you might end up leading trainings."

"Huh?"

"It's what Tyler said. The training never

ends."

And then—the train moved. Slowly at first, but picking up speed. We fumbled for our seatbelts.

FIVE

The train doesn't move fast.

It's not designed for that. It's designed for safety. Every hull, every deck, every piece of equipment is studded with monitors. There are several thousand sensors in every car that all have to vote yes before the train can move.

But we moved fast enough.

We rolled for a while, we rolled across the dark landscapes of South Dakota, it felt like forever, but it was only a few minutes. Finally we saw a blaze of lights illuminating huge overhead frameworks, cranes, and gantries. A few kilometers farther and we rolled into a long cylindrical tunnel, dark at first, then it became brighter. Pipes and tubes and cables lined the walls, monitors and sensors studded everything.

Then we rolled into a bright section where everything dazzled.

We felt the gravitational change immediately.

It was like that first drop on a roller coaster —sudden enough to cause an involuntary yelp. We never quite settled into the bottom though. We felt . . . I don't know how to describe it. Lighter.

The train slowed, almost stopping while we rolled through the long airlock, no atmospheric leakage from the Earth, then finally we came out of the tube and the screens that served as windows blazed. The sun-dazzled Lunar landscape glittered, everything so bright, and the horizon almost close enough to touch.

Our hearts pounded for a moment, a long moment, many long moments—as long as it took for our bodies to adjust to Luna's one-sixth Earth gravity. Or maybe it was just the excitement.

Alec was grinning. "That first bounce. It always gets you. Every time. No matter how much you expect it, it's still unexpected."

"*Madre de dios*," gasped José. "We're on the moon." He pointed toward one of the screens that served as windows. Outside, the uneven Lunar plain, dazzling white in places where the hills shone in the sun, painful dark where it was pocked with craters, some of them huge. The track stretched across the landscape, curving around the bigger holes, and heading somewhere beyond the too-near horizon.

We made appreciative noises. We said words that would have been curses anywhere else, but here were exclamations of astonishment. We poked each other and pointed at the biggest craters, the hills and rills and unexplainable geologies—no, geo meant Earth. Selenologies. Luna.

We marveled at the brightness of the landscape, the darkness of the sky, until we ran out of words and just stared in awe. There was nothing else to say. It was beautiful and desolate, magnificent and disturbing.

José squeezed my hand. "*Esto es real.*"

"*Si*," I agreed. "*Muy.*"

After a moment, in English, he said, "We're really here. We're really here, aren't we?"

"You can't fake the gravity," I said. "*Esto es real.*"

Finally, we sat back in our seats and looked across at Alec and Tyler and Hunter. "Wow," I said. Tyler laughed. Hunter was still too awestruck to say much. "I dreamt of this," he said softly. "I never thought I'd ever . . ." He trailed off.

"Yeah," agreed Alec. "Yeah. Everybody gets that. It's the shock. The realization. The reality. The moment. I still get it. There's something amazing about this place. Undefinable." He added, "There'll be a stopover at Luna City—officially, it's Armstrong Station, but neither the Russians nor the Chinese have accepted that name, so . . . okay. Whatever. You'll have some time to explore. Twelve hours at least. The mechanics will check the integrity of every car of every train before they let them go on. There isn't the same quality of service further up the line."

"How likely is a delay?"

Alec shook his head. "Not very. If anything serious needs to be replaced or repaired, they'll swap in a replacement car. Mostly it's just routine service. If you want, you can go to the observatory at Turtledome, you'll have time, it's only thirty minutes away. They have the big scope, sometimes they point it at Earth, but you can see most of that online. I think you'll find Luna City more interesting. Take a walk, look around. See as much as you can." He added, "It's a long trip. Use it to see how different each world is. But watch the time. You'll have to be back on the train an hour before departure."

We nodded our agreement.

"Oh, another thing," he said. "You'll have to learn how to walk in Lunar gravity. It's a skill, not hard to learn, but newbies always think it's fun to bounce—until the second or third time you hit the overhead, but you gotta get it out of your system quickly. The locals don't like it." He paused, took a breath and started again slower. "Walking is applied physics. You lean forward and you keep putting your feet ahead of you so you don't fall. On Earth, you don't have to lean very far. On Luna, well, you'll see. It's kind of funny to see people leaning so far forward just to move. But you get used to it quickly."

Alec unbuckled himself and demonstrated how to walk, up the aisle and back. He was right. It looked funny, but it worked. One at a time, the rest of us practiced too. It felt weird—well, it was weird. We learned how to shuffle and bounce and move with what felt like baby steps. But it worked. As long as we paid attention to what we were doing, we didn't bounce. Well, not too high.

When he was satisfied we could walk without injuring ourselves or denting the bulkheads, he sat us down again. "You want to be very careful with liquids. Your coffee will bounce right out of your cup, that's why loonies put a lid on everything. Everything. Oh, and you should sit to pee. At least until you get the hang of it. You'll notice the toilets are shaped like funnels. Because things splatter higher here. And walk—walk a lot. So your bowels get enough exercise. Anything else you need to know, there'll be signs and labels. Read them."

We rolled into a long airlock, then a second one, a third one as well, and finally into the terminal. They weren't taking chances here. The Montana blowout had scared everybody, up and down the entire line.

We got off the train and gathered on the platform, all hundred and thirty-two of us who'd boarded the train to Praxis. Quickly, our team leaders separated us into groups of three or four, no more than that, and sent us off in different directions to explore loonie-town.

Luna City declared independence during the great political reformation of the thirties. The corporate entities that controlled the three superpowers had been too concerned with earthbound concerns, assuming they'd deal with Luna's independence later. But the loonies said they'd shut down all inbound and outbound traffic if their autonomy was threatened. If necessary, they'd even close the portals to Earth.

And . . . because there were several orbital portals and a few others scattered around the solar system to facilitate interplanetary traffic, it would be no small matter to drop rocks from space. You don't want to go to war against an enemy who has unlimited high ground.

It wasn't exactly the end of corporatism—it was simply a change of management. But the loonies had a different ideology. They regarded greed and selfishness as mortal sins. A community only survives when it takes care of all its members. And most of the portal worlds followed that lead.

José and I had talked about it a few times. Where does ideology collide with morality? Or pragmatism? Or maybe just empathy? How do we think globally, but act locally? José said it was simple. "Don't be a *pendejo*." After I thought about it, I figured he was right. Human beings don't need more ideology than that.

SIX

Most of Luna City was underground, a long lava tube that stretched down into the crust. According to one of the information plaques, lava tubes are formed when molten lava flows beneath a field of cooled lava, or a crust forms over a river of lava. Lunar lava tubes are usually formed on sloped surfaces that range from half a degree to seven degrees. Some of the tubes are as wide as half a kilometer. This was Luna City.

The walls of this lava tube had been reinforced and sealed to be airtight. It was a long linear town with a tram running down the center. Occasional tunnels had been dug out, branching off into habitats or farms.

Structures here, I guess you could call them buildings, looked like a jumble of disjointed blocks. There are things you can do in one-sixth gravity that you wouldn't even suggest at one-gee. Frameworks that looked too spindly to be strong enough reached nearly to the roof of the tube.

Many were hung with banners, some had parts closed off, a few others had hanging balconies, sometimes with lavish gardens. But more than a few had been built for emergency survival—in the "unlikely" case of a blow-out. We saw airlocks everywhere, some private but most marked with yellow alert signs. This was a rigorous environment. Real loonies did not take chances.

Less rigorous structures, mostly shops and restaurants and a few businesses existed below as booths or compartments, mostly defined by simple partitions, but sometimes just colorful drapes hanging from a frame. We saw no billboards, no huge signs, only polite banners and occasional public service booths.

Oh, and gardens everywhere--trees of all kinds, flower gardens and rose bushes, trellises with walls of colorful bougainvillea climbing higher than they ever could have on Earth. Giant Hanging flower boxes, sported bits of unkempt wilderness. Butterflies and bees hovered in the air. I wondered what they thought of Luna's lesser gravity.

The air smelled surprisingly fresh. We had expected the usual medicinal stink of refreshers, but no—Luna had a policy of having at least five times as much area set aside for farms as for living space. Fresh air was more valuable than water here.

Overhead, huge lamps blazed with artificial daylight. Everything dazzled with bright colors.

Luna was on Greenwich standard time and we had arrived just before lunch. Amazing smells greeted us, coming from restaurants and florist shops and flower gardens.

After Earth, after the training sessions, Luna looked like paradise.

It wasn't, of course. Loonies had to exercise two or three times a day, just to keep from losing bone and muscle mass. Vitamins and protein supplements were mandatory. Loonies had to spend regular hours in a centrifuge if they ever planned to visit Earth. Their health was so rigorously monitored by the local networks, they couldn't be pre-diabetic or at risk for a heart attack without immediate warnings. A lot of elderly people believed that getting away from Earth's gravity would prolong their lives—but not many could make the trip. Emigration here was limited and expensive. Luna couldn't afford a surplus of non-productive citizens, so residency was strictly limited.

But it could afford tourists, lots of them. A weekend on Luna wasn't prohibitively expensive, no more than a weekend in Vegas or Miami. And Luna was a chance to experience something radically different—wearing a spacesuit, exploring a nearby crater, making footprints in the dust, seeing the stars without an atmosphere in the way—and inside, all the low-gee adventures like soaring and swimming, and especially low-gee sex, all of it. Especially the sex. Tourists from

Earth were Luna's biggest business. They were a significant part of the Lunar economy and serving them was a lucrative career.

José and I followed Alec, Tyler, and Hunter to a Japanese restaurant Alec recommended. We had sushi and tempura and ramen and things I couldn't identify, but they were delicious.

Most of Luna's food was now grown locally, even some of the fish, but there were still a lot of items that had to be brought up from Earth. Almost every train arrived with necessary stores and supplies, especially foods from Earth that Luna couldn't provide.

In return, Luna sent back products that could only be manufactured in vacuum, like microchips. And vacuum balls that floated in the Earth's air. And moon rocks too. Lots of people on Earth wanted moon rocks—worthless as rocks, but great as collectibles. Oh, and low-gravity bread, it rises more, it gets fluffier in low-gee, and cake becomes an airy confection.

We laughed in surprise. Tyler shoved a piece of cake into Hunter's face. Hunter kissed him back, smearing cake over both their faces.

I looked at José, surprised.

SEVEN

José and I went back to our cabin early.

We needed to talk.

Alone.

We sat on the bed again.

"Did you see Tyler and Hunter? The way they fed each other cake?"

José nodded. "They're a couple now. Everybody knows that."

"That's not what I'm talking about. The way they talked, they're . . . they're going to do it. Low-gee . . . um, you know."

José looked at me, his expression was serious. "You don't like talking about sex, do you?"

I swallowed hard. "I guess it's part of having it turned off. They were laughing. They looked happy." I looked down at the deck. "Joyous. I didn't know that was possible. Like that."

"It is," said José. He reached over and took my hand.

"I guess so. Um. I was looking at things. Looking things up. There are . . . services here.

Girls. Boys. They're licensed. And I thought . . . if you wanted to, I mean, how often do you get a chance to experience low-gee coupling, if that's something you wanted to experience, that would be all right with me."

José's expression went from amusement to serious. He squeezed my hand tight, but his tone went hard. "I suppose I should appreciate the generosity of that thought, the way you think. But maybe I should be insulted too—that you would think I might want that."

"I don't understand."

"No, you don't. That's why I'm upset." He let go of my hand. "Yes, I've heard that low-gee sex is different and fun and worth the trip to Luna, but real sex requires a real partner, Jamie. Sex with someone you don't know—that whole business of being physically intimate with a stranger—it's empty. It's incomplete. I've done it. It doesn't feel right. And I'm really sad that you suggested it, because—because it almost feels like a betrayal. I mean, I'm trying to figure this out that maybe you can't understand, because you had it turned off. But me, over here, I couldn't do it with anyone else. Because you're my husband."

I looked at my feet. I was wearing the soft indoor slippers we had been issued when we boarded. They looked silly. And I felt a hot flush of shame.

"I screwed it up, didn't I?"

He didn't answer immediately. He sighed.

He said, "You didn't mean to."

"José," I said. "I'm sorry. I just—" I swallowed hard. Even harder this time. It hurt to speak. "I just want you to be happy and—"

"I am happy," he said. He squeezed my hand hard. "I'm happy with you. And I should appreciate it that you were thinking of me. But . . . dammit, I wish you hadn't turned yourself off. I wish you could understand what it means to be partners physically."

I nodded silently.

"I do love you jay-man," he said. "I really do."

"I love you too."

"But—? What is it? What is it you're not saying?"

It hurt to speak. "I just keep wondering if maybe somehow we're not complete."

"Is that it? Is that really it?"

"Uh-huh."

José took a breath, made a decision, then he pushed me down onto the bed and stretched out on top of me. He felt so light. Lunar gravity. Interesting. I had to put my hands on his shoulders to hold him in place. Before I could say anything about that, he kissed me, shyly at first, then . . . completely. He took his time. After a bit, I kissed him back. I took my time too. It was . . . nice.

He looked at me. "Do you want more? Or do you want to stop?"

I thought about it. "It was nice."

"Do you want more?"

"There's more?"

"You really don't know?"

"Um, this is hard for me to say, but, um, yes . . . I think I'd like to know."

"You think?"

"I want to know. I just don't know if I'm ready."

José squeezed my hand. "Nobody is ever ready for the future. We learned that in the training. Remember?"

I nodded.

"So, you want to know? I do too. Let's find out."

I took a breath. "Okay."

"Okay," José said, lifting himself up. "If you want to get turned on, I will get turned on with you. And if you want to do it here—I think we still have time." He bounced to his feet. Literally. "Let's go find a psychomat. Or whatever they call it here."

"You're really sure about this?" I said. One last chance to back out.

He gave me that look. The one that meant he was through talking.

"Okay," I said, following him out the door. "Okay."

EIGHT

I got turned on.

José got recalibrated.

It didn't take long.

When it was over, we looked at each other differently. And we laughed.

"I don't feel any different," I said.

"Me neither."

"They said it takes a while."

"Uh-huh."

"We shouldn't rush it."

"Yeah. Except—"

"What?"

"We're only gonna be here a few hours more. Let's rush it."

We walked around for a while, holding hands, doing some of the obvious tourist things, waiting for whatever it was we were waiting for. Finally, we stopped stalling and went back to our cabin.

It wasn't perfect. It was clumsy. We didn't know what we were doing. We fumbled around a lot. But it was fantastic.

Afterward, afterward . . . lying together, floating naked together in a haze of strange, wonderful emotions, I said, "Yeah, okay. That was good. I liked it."

José laughed. And then I laughed, realizing how silly I sounded. And then he laughed because I was bouncing up and down on him. And then he lifted me up over his head, it wasn't hard in Lunar gee, he looked into my eyes and said, "Yeah, okay." And we laughed a lot more. And then we wrapped ourselves up in each other and just rested.

Finally, after a long while, José lifted himself up on one arm and looked at me. "So I guess we're ready for Praxis now."

We took a shower together, that was fun too, pulled on shirts and shorts, and headed for the lounge. Alec, Tyler, Hunter, and a few others had already scattered themselves around the cabin. Tyler looked at us speculatively, turned to Hunter. "Yep, you were right."

"Huh?"

"We're a small town," said Hunter.

Alec explained. "They were wondering when you two would figure it out."

"Get it on," said Hunter.

José looked embarrassed. "Is it that obvious?"

Tyler pointed. "Jamie is smiling."

Oh. I hadn't realized.

"Welcome to the club."

"Huh? It's a club?"

"It's a figure of speech," said José. "He meant you're human again."

"I've always been human," I said. "I just haven't been . . . complete."

"I like your smile," he said.

"Me too. From the inside."

I didn't say much more. I guess that was something else to think about. Some emotions could be visible. José dragged me to the galley and we got ourselves sandwiches and drinks, then returned to the lounge.

While we waited for the chime, we shared our experiences of Luna City, what we saw, what we did, who we met, what we learned, what we discovered. There were things we didn't share, of course, especially José and me, but most of it was pretty interesting.

Almost everybody had gone to the sky room to look at the Earth, the big blue marble. It was both bigger and smaller than I expected. I'd seen pictures. This was different. *Esto es real*—a sparkling globe, one half sunlit and glowing blue, the other half in shadow, but glittering with the lights of fabled cities.

There are no words for it. The experience is amazing and awesome and humbling and exhilarating and even a little sad, I'm not sure why. But completely overwhelming. Some of our people broke down crying. I came away speechless. But like thousands of others before us, we had to agree that seeing Earth from Luna this way was a magnificent rush of emotions.

Later, after the obligatory visit to the view, others sampled the other experiences of low-gee. Some visited the sensory deprivation tanks where they could float suspended on a warm solution of Epson salt and water. You could do that on Earth, but in low-gee it's supposed to be a kind of weightlessness. José and I had passed.

Tyler and Hunter went to a low-gee gymnasium and bounced around the high-frames, but Alec went flying. He did that every trip he could, but this would be his last chance. There's a chamber where tourists can rent powered wingsuits. Resident loonies have leagues and play a variation of soccer. But even in Lunar-gee, flying can be dangerous, it's not recommended for the inexperienced. Like tourists.

"But then how do you get experience?"

"Training sessions. Everything is training. Everything in life. From the day you're born, everything is training. You learn to walk, you learn to use a fork, you learn to read and write. You learn some manners. Most people get that far, they think they're done. That's when they start to fossilize. But real people are never done training. You have to choose who you want to be, because you're the author of your life."

"You're doing it again," said Hunter, grinning. "Being a trainer."

"Everybody's a trainer," said Alec, grinning

back. "But most people don't know it. It's sad. They're missing the best part of the adventure."

NINE

The chime sounded then. A moment later the train began to move. The window-screens showed us moving through a series of tunnels and airlocks and finally out onto the Lunar surface again. Bright magnificent desolation, a sharp horizon, a dark black sky. The glare from the sun made it hard to make out the stars.

"This leg of the trip will be longer, we'll be crossing the terminator and heading around to the back side. It'll be dark, so you'll get to see the stars like you've never seen them before. But it'll be a few hours, so you should get some rest while you can." He added, "From here on out, we won't have a regular day-night schedule. You'll have to monitor yourselves. Make sure you schedule enough gym time."

It was obvious Alec was dismissing us back to our cabins. José and I didn't object, we were feeling over-stimulated and exhausted. It was all too much, too fast—especially the emotional part.

We crawled into bed, just held onto each other. We must have fallen asleep in that position because that was our position when we drifted back to wakefulness.

I turned on the screens that showed us the view outside. The landscape was dark, but the train had lights, bright lights, illuminating the terrain around us. It was mostly the same, but different. The far side of Luna has a very different topography, a lot more impact craters, very few flat areas, marias that astronomers sometimes call seas.

And then there's the sky.

Luna doesn't have an atmosphere. The little there is, is insignificant, almost immeasurable, so the Lunar sky is the clearest and brightest possible view of the Milky Way anywhere short of deep space. From horizon to horizon, the universe glimmers with light—a spectacle of light that has taken years, even centuries to arrive here.

José asked me how I knew so much. I told him the truth. When you don't have any friends, you hide out in books. Movies, videos of all kinds, and computer games. Anything that lets you avoid other people.

"So you're going to get stupid around me now?" he joked.

"Well . . . if being stupid is as much fun as last night—"

He blushed. I laughed. He laughed.

"Can I ask you something?"

"Anything, I guess."

"Have you ever been tested for neuro-divergence?"

"Um . . ."

"And . . . ?"

I took a breath. "I'm obsessive-compulsive, sort of. I have to have things be complete, so I read every book and watch every episode in a series. I have to have complete sets of things. If there's something I have to know, I can spend days doing research. So, um, also, I'm kinda neuro-divergent, a little. But that's a bad assessment, I think, because everyone is neuro-divergent, because there's no such thing as neuro-typical, just a big lumpy stew for people who haven't been measured. Supposedly, I have a genius IQ, but you couldn't prove it by my life. And I've probably got some post-traumatic stress from . . . I dunno. Just growing up."

José looked sad. "You were bullied?"

"Wasn't everyone? Life is a bully."

I took another breath, much longer this time. "I always thought if I were as smart as all those tests showed that I'd be able to figure things out and be a winner. So I read a lot. But I guess I was so smart in the wrong way that I was actually stupid."

"You're not stupid," he said.

"I don't know," I said. "Everybody around me seems to know things I don't. I've pretended to be normal, even around you, but—"

José put a finger across my lips to silence me. He pulled me close into a hug. I didn't pull back. I actually liked it. He held on for a long time.

"Why are you so good to me?" I finally asked.

"I dunno. It seemed like a good idea at the time."

I stared at him. "That was a joke, yes?"

He grinned. "Yes, that was a joke. Yes."

"What's the real reason?"

"I fell in love. I didn't think I'd ever fall in love again. But I did. So . . . there you are. You're stuck with me."

"Okay," I said.

"Okay," he said back.

We showered and went to the lounge for breakfast.

TEN

The window-displays in the lounge showed a thin line of light stretching up out of the darkness, disappearing somewhere above. The Lunar Beanstalk. I hadn't expected we'd be able to see it, but it was so brightly illuminated up and down its entire length that it was visible almost everywhere on the far side.

Someone pressed for magnification and we could see the capsules riding up and down its length. They were the same pill-shaped vehicles that made up our train, only vertical. It was a convenient construction.

"It looks pretty busy," Tyler said.

"Uh-huh." Alec came up behind him. "It's the most active orbital elevator in the entire system. It's also the only one. So far." He explained. "Those capsules? They get released outward. Most contain telescopes. We're turning the solar system into a giant eye on the universe. A lot of the units are simply signal repeaters to facilitate interworld communications. There are a lot of other monitors and probes too. All kinds. We're sending out hundreds of eyes and ears every month." He paused for effect. "But some of them are shipping proto-portals."

"Proto-portals?"

"Uh-huh. They'll take a while getting to their final destinations, planets or moons or orbital locations—when they arrive onsite, the engineers open the proto-portal, secure it, and eventually a station is pushed through. If the destination is a planet or a moon, they'll push through a landing engine and take it down. Eventually, when confidence is high enough, the portal is opened to traffic and the human race gets immediate access to wherever the portal has been located. In the next decade we could be setting up stations on Mercury, Ganymede, Titan, Europa, Ceres, and after that, Pluto and Sedna and as much of the Oort Cloud as we want— the entire solar system really. But we can't get there until the portals are set up. The beanstalk is the most economical way of launching them. Any questions?"

There were questions, a lot, but we were distracted by another installation. "Oh," said Alec. "That's the most amazing one. It's the base station for an interstellar tractor drive."

"Huh? What?"

"You put a station in orbit with a traction drive and fuel tanks. You attach a portal to it. You launch it toward a nearby star. As the fuel is used up, you pump more through the portal. You get constant acceleration without a weight penalty, so that portal is going to reach nearly one-third light speed. It'll reach Proxima Centauri sometime in the next twenty years. It's out beyond Pluto already and still boosting. If this one works, if long distance portals are practical, and the engineers think they are, the math is good, then the grand plan is to use the portals to leapfrog to the stars. What you're looking at over there is the fuel pumping station for the Daedalus probe."

"Oh, wow."

"Yes, that's what most people say."

We stopped just long enough to release the last car from the train, supplies for the station, then rolled on. We gathered around the display, watching the station until it disappeared beneath the Lunar horizon behind us. It wasn't all that impressive, it looked like most other Lunar installations, just a lot of domes and tanks and communication discs, but somehow this one was special.

"Why don't they launch the proto-portals the same way?"

Alec shook his head. "It's not cost-effective to build that kind of engine for every probe. And even if it were, we don't have the people or the equipment to activate every portal right away. We'll put through probes first and monitor the conditions and establish transit stations when we have the resources. Or when we can sell licenses. These are all long-term plans. The Transit Authority is still working on how to make the economics work. And the politics. There's a lot of money involved."

He stopped himself. "The real challenge will be us. Becoming a species that's worthy of the stars." He shook his head. "Sometimes I have my doubts. But . . . what's that thing Mr. Short says? Don't be the darkness, be a lantern. Light the way." He looked at the time. "Right. I talk too much. It's a bad habit. We call it Trainer Syndrome. Sorry about that—"

"No, it was fascinating."

"Thank you. But we have to stay on schedule. We'll be transiting to Mars in a bit. You might want to strap in. You'll feel the shift. You'll have to learn to walk again. Martian gravity is one-third gee, twice that of Luna."

A few minutes later, we entered the airlocks. The displays turned orange.

And we were on Mars.

ELEVEN

We had another half-day on Mars for another set of service checks, plus delivery of cargo. Bradbury City was nowhere near as expansive as Luna City, but it was well serviced and once again, the food was excellent. The cakes weren't as fluffy, but they were easier to eat. They didn't fall apart in our hands.

The view was spectacular for a while . . . until it got boring.

But after sunset—

The night sky on Mars is almost as spectacular as Luna's. Mars has enough gravity to hold an atmosphere, but not much of one, a hundred times less dense than the atmosphere of Earth, not enough to dull the view. The stars shine brighter. The Milky Way sprawls across the sky. It's very romantic. If you want it to be.

We did.

Martian sex is better than Lunar sex. Gravity is essential to good coupling. I liked José's weight. I wondered if it would be even better in near-Earth gee. Well, I'd find out when we reached Praxis.

The train had to go around Olympus Mons, the giant volcano that bulges out of the surface of the planet, three times as high as Everest and as wide as Texas. After the expected, almost mandatory, oohing and aahhing over the scenery, the endless red and orange and brown desolation, we got bored and went to the gym where we ran on treadmills for half an hour. Martian gravity makes running easier, so you have to run harder to get the same exercise benefit. Afterward, a hot shower, with water drops falling slowly onto you is like a gentle massage. José and I agreed that we liked it better than Lunar showers, because the water behaved more like we were used to. On Luna, the water bounces around a lot.

After Mars, we transited to an airless asteroid. It was named after some forgotten American president. Alec said it was somebody's idea of a joke. The rock was useless, except as a steppingstone to better places. From there, an ice world where several stations carved up blocks of frozen methane for export to industrial stations.

After that, the dark side of a barren desert world, too close to its primary. We were nowhere near the terminator. Alec acknowledged that we were no longer in any known space. When a portal is opened randomly, it might not even be in our own universe. Nobody knows for sure, the math doesn't resolve easily. There are theories. José didn't understand them either.

A few more transits and José and I got bored with the route map. Most of the stations on this branch were industrial. We delivered supplies to most of them, and some places we had a short layover before moving on. But none of these stations were as welcoming as Luna City or Bradbury. They were industrial sites, not tourist destinations. They had the necessary comforts for the resident workers, but few facilities for travelers.

We almost got used to the sudden shifts in gravity every time we transited. Actually, we got bored with them. We'd hear a chime, we'd sit in the nearest chair, fasten our seatbelts, and wait. Even when we knew what was coming, it was always a physical shock. Like a roller coaster or a drop tower. Annoying or exhilarating, depending on whatever we were feeling, whatever had been interrupted.

Some worlds were heavy, not many though, some were light, and some were so insignificant we might as well have been in free fall. That was why we needed the seatbelts. Tumbling from weightlessness to a one-gee world can be painful. We heard that a couple of guys in another car didn't strap down and suffered cracked ribs.

Every world was different, each in its own way. Some were too bright, too close to their suns, some were so far out they were perpetually dark, their suns were just bright stars in the sky.

But each time, we crowded around the window-displays, because every new world was beautiful in its own way—but it was a strange ugly kind of beauty, desolate and magnificent and even a little scary. There aren't a lot of livable worlds out here, are there? We have to bring our safe environments with us.

José and I mostly kept to ourselves. We weren't the only ones. A lot of the guys hung out in the gym. It was something to do as we rolled carefully from one portal to the next. We delivered mail and supplies and sometimes cargo. Sometimes we stopped for a bit, sometimes we just kept rolling.

We did what we could to keep from getting bored. Some of the guys started a poker tournament, others played dominos or cribbage. Some immersed themselves in books or videos. One of the cars set up a dance floor and we heard rumors that some of the guys had planned low-gee orgies. Whatever.

José and I went to the gym and walked the treadmills even when we didn't have to. The screens showed us scenery, sometimes places on Earth, sometimes places on other worlds. Whatever we wanted. Mostly we walked because it was something to do, a way to alleviate not just the restlessness of our bodies, but the restlessness of our spirits as well.

It felt like we existed in an endless limbo, waiting for something to happen—and afraid that

it would.
       It did.

TWELVE

Maybe someday, some future historian will read this account and say, "Well, finally."

Because maybe some future historian will be so familiar with travel between portals, with the landscapes of Luna and Mars and all the transit worlds beyond, that all of the previous accounts will seem boring and annoying, just another time-wasting travelogue.

So what?

I'm not writing for history. I'm writing what happened, what we saw, what we felt, and, how the world worked when we lived in it.

All of this was new to us, and I only began this account as a personal journal, a way to remember what we were going through and what we were feeling along the way.

Until it happened.

And everything changed.

The train was stalled on a siding. The gravity was a half-gee, this rock was dark and barren, somewhere in the local equivalent of an asteroid belt. The displays showed a broken gloomy landscape and a glistening backdrop of stars.

We unloaded supplies at the transit station, but we didn't move on. Maintenance check? Maybe. But a little while stretched into a long while . . . and then then a longer while. By the time anyone noticed, Alec had disappeared into his cabin, with a do-not-disturb flag on the door.

So we went to the lounge and waited. And speculated. And convinced ourselves that it was nothing to worry about, or maybe something so horrendous nobody even knew how to report it.

Until finally Alec returned. He signaled all of the other cars in the train, "Please come and gather in our lounge."

It took a while. A hundred other men had to pass through multiple airlocks, only five at a time. But ultimately, all of us were crowded side by side into a single lounge.

Alec didn't answer any questions. Instead, he gave us some very strange instructions. "Please turn off all your electronics." He waited. While he waited for assurances, he set out several portable lanterns, turning each one on. Finally, he did something to one of the control panels and the lounge went dark.

The whole car went dark.

Only the light from the lanterns remained. We existed as shadowy faces floating in a void.

"I can't be sure we're air-gapped," Alec said, his voice unnaturally loud. "But I have to try. I'll tell you what you what I know and I'm going to trust all of you to keep this to yourselves. Our safety might depend upon it. Is there anyone who cannot agree to that? If so, I'll ask you to leave."

Nobody left. Alec took that as consent.

"All right," he said. "Here's what I've been able to find out. Please listen carefully. Apparently something has happened on Praxis. Nobody is certain. All communication has been cut off. We know that the portals are still open, all the way up the line, all the way to the fringes, but there have been no responses to any of our messages to the Praxis portal station and no messages from anything beyond. They've gone completely dark."

He paused for a moment, waiting while that part sunk in. "Here's what we do know. Praxis has been in political turmoil for a week. Something happened while we've been traveling. We're not sure what. Only that the last message out of Praxis was a demand for all traffic to stop. I've sent a note downline, asking for advice and instructions. They don't know any more than we do. Our instructions are to hold position and wait for further instructions." He held up a hand, a barely visible movement in the darkness. "No, I don't know how long. We can stay parked here for a couple months if we have to. Whatever has happened up there, they will want our supplies. So we shouldn't be stalled too long, but if they tell us we can proceed . . . we won't know what we'll find up there."

THIRTEEN

For a while, we talked, we speculated, we imagined, we surmised, we suggested, we considered possibilities—we talked until there was nothing left to say. I knew what Alec was doing. He was letting us "empty the cup." He was letting us vent until we had nothing left to say. But we said it three or four times before Alec finally said, "All right, let's stop here. Go back to the galley or the gym or your cabins and talk about everything but this. Please. Leave all your theories and assumptions and opinions here. You know how to do it. I know it's not easy, but lets treat it like one of those exercises where you're not allowed to talk. As soon as there's anything to report, we'll meet again here."

A pudgy fellow named Matthew raised his hand. "Um—one question. Isn't it a little strange that we're meeting like this?" He indicated the dark cabin around us. "Air-gapped? At least, we think we're air-gapped."

Alec nodded. "It's not unusual for emigres to

have private meetings. But yes, you're right. The circumstances are suspicious. But we are our own group. This meeting is for us. So let's not discuss it outside, okay?"

And with that we broke up.

José and I considered the galley. Coffee and sandwiches, a lot of things we might never have again, but neither of us felt like being around other people, so we just went back to our cabin and crawled into bed and held onto each other for a while. "Let's talk about us," said José. "Are you okay?"

"I'm fine," I said.

"No. I mean, with us. With this." He hugged me tight for a moment.

"Oh," I said. "I think so. Yes. I'm just . . . I still have to figure it all out. Except there's nothing to figure out, is there? Or is there?" I had to ask. shifted my position so I could see his face. "Are you okay?"

José nodded. "*Si*. I think so. *Es diferente*. But nice. Maybe even . . . better, kinda. I dunno. Maybe I'm feeling the recalibration?" He hesitated. "But, yeah, *esta bien*. I'm good."

We lay there silently for a while.

Finally, I said, "José?"

"Jamie?"

I cleared my throat. "I think I'm comfortable. With you. I don't know if I've ever been comfortable with anyone before. This is all new to me. But I like it so far. Is that okay?"

Next to me, I felt him nod. "Uh-huh. I think so. Me too."

And that was all either of us had to say about that.

So we lay there in silence. Maybe that was part of it too. Just being together without having to say anything.

We must have drifted off to sleep. I woke up only because I had to pee. And after I came back to bed, José got up groggily and staggered to the head. He came back, slightly refreshed. He'd splashed his face with water. "Are we rolling again?"

I nodded. "I think so. Only backwards. We're going back down."

José checked our messages. "There's a meeting in an hour. Just enough time for coffee and a bite."

It wasn't a great breakfast, but it was enough. We gathered in the lounge and waited while the rest airlocked in. This time, Alec had arranged portable lamps, so we weren't gathered in gloom.

"Yes, we're rolling," he began. "The engineers are moving us two stops downline to a larger industrial station. It's very low-gee, but it's well-equipped, they do hospitality from time to time when trains get stalled. They know we're coming, it's all arranged. You'll be able to disembark to use their facilities, showers, gym, running track, but you'll return to your cabins for sleeping and you'll still take your meals in your respective galleys. Oh, and you'll want to wear grip shoes, not all the overheads are padded. They'll partition a space we can use for our meetings. We'll pay for their hospitality with some of our extra cargo. Maybe we can bill it to Praxis. I'll know more later."

He waited until the murmurs of agreement died down. "There's something else. We're not sure yet what it means, but the portal to Praxis has picked up a very, very slight flutter. It's almost undetectable, but the portal engineers noticed it this morning and they're running system checks. Maybe it doesn't mean anything. Maybe it's just a reflection of something in the local power supply. But I promise to keep you informed, so let's hold off on any chatter until we get to North Station. Right? Thanks. Lunch will be early, but it won't be fancy."

FOURTEEN

North Station was a low-gravity rock, tumbling around an unstable blue primary, but enough of it had been hollowed out that after our long trip in the cargo train it felt roomy. And we had time to discover how everything worked. The low-gee, however . . .

We were given a perfunctory tour, with a promise for more detailed excursions later, when we got our space legs. We were led—no, we bounced like clumsy water balloons down to where most of the long-term facilities were located, just in case the local star erupted.

The portal engineers had a theory that a pass-around route might one day be possible, but right now North Station was valuable for its industrial facilities. The station exported bubbles of 100% pure vacuum, or close enough to 100% that the far side of the decimal point was irrelevant.

We settled ourselves into a rough schedule for the gym and the showers and waited. North

Station had bandwidth all the way down, so Alec conferred at length with everyone who might be able to offer assistance, the train crew, Portal Authorities, Line Management, every affected station, and our own Immigration Agency as well. Several thousand people were examining the situation, everything anybody knew, but nobody had any answers.

After those discussions were exhausted, Alec always came back and reported. Except there wasn't anything new to report. "We're still studying the situation," was not reassuring. "Until Praxis starts returning our signals, we can't move forward. And as you already know, the only instructions we're getting from downline is that we should hold position and wait. But Praxis is going to need our cargo soon. They'll have to reopen the portal."

"And then what?"

Alec shrugged. "Nobody knows. It depends on who we're talking to. Do we shut down the supply lines? Or do we grant them legitimacy and go back to work? The corporations are only looking at their bottom line. The human rights agencies are looking at . . . well, human rights."

"There are no human rights," muttered someone in the back. "There never have been. Only corporate interests. We're all slaves to the system. That's why most of us are here. The alternative was the Labor Corps." Murmurs of resentful agreement followed.

Alec held up a hand for silence. "Me too," he said.

And that stopped everyone. This was the first time he'd ever discussed his own past.

Alec swallowed hard and looked around at all of us. Some were hanging from straps on what would have been the ceiling, if we'd had gravity. Others were perched around the walls at odd angles.

"I'm under the same contract," he said. "So you don't have to convince me that the whole situation is unfair. I've already had that conversation. More than once. And I don't like it any more than you do. But here we are anyway. This is the choice we made, this is the place we arrived at, this is it, this is what we get to deal with. And whatever happens, I'm in it with you. And no, I'm not having any fun either."

That last sentence got a laugh, not a big one, but enough to lighten the mood a little.

"On the other hand," he said, ". . . being here might still be better than being there. For now, at least."

That got a few chuckles. And a few frustrated head shakes. As a team, most of us had moved beyond frustration and annoyance to sheer boredom. It wasn't good for morale. Alec was doing his best, we knew that, but his regular reports that we were still stuck in amber, or worse, slowly fossilizing, had become a source of bleak humor. "I notta like this Wednesday," was a common remark. "We ever gonna have Thursday?"

By the third day, attendance at the meetings had fallen off. Only thirty or forty of us showed up. José and I went only because it was a break in the day.

"I do have some news. I'm not sure what it means, feel free to speculate, you're going to do that anyway. But here it is. You might remember I said that the portal engineers had noticed a very slight flutter in the system. It might be a deliberate modulation. If it is, and if they can decode it, then it might be a signal. It might give us a clue as to what's going on up there. Or it might be . . ." he shrugged, "just an artifact of their power supply. We should know more in a few hours. If it's anything at all, as soon as I have something to report, I will."

FIFTEEN

Alec took a few questions. José and I didn't stay for the rest. We went to the gym and walked on the treadmills for an hour or so. We put on helmets, listened to music and watched VR videos of imaginary paths to follow. The treadmills exercised our arms and our legs together and sometimes required that we speed up to exercise our hearts. In low-gee, it was easy to just go through the motions, but both José and I used the treadmills to work off our growing annoyance and frustration and whatever other emotions were building up inside us. We had agreed we would stay on the treadmills until we were too physically exhausted to do anything else—what some people called "the magnificent emptiness," but what we called, "too tired to die."

Afterward, the showers—which weren't really showers at all, just hoses with spray nozzles in a watertight chamber, lined with some pretty serious suction to catch all the bouncing droplets. Sometimes, José sprayed me, sometimes I sprayed him, but today we showered separately, not talking at all.

When we returned to our cabin on the train, I started crying.

José tried to put his arm around my shoulder, but I shook him off. "I'm sorry," I said. "I don't know how to do this. I don't even know who I am anymore."

He waited for me to say more. I just shook my head and sobbed.

"I don't know where I am. I don't know how we got here. I thought it would be all right, all the training, everything, you—especially you—but—" I sniffled a glob of snot and wiped my face on my sleeve. "I don't know anything, José. I'm sorry."

"Yeah, me neither."

"What we do together, I like it. But afterward, I'm lying there, staring at the overhead, wondering what just happened, because it isn't like anything, it isn't me anymore, and I don't know if that's who I want to be because I don't know how to be that person and I don't want to make you unhappy, but sometimes I'm wondering if I made a mistake, do you ever feel that way . . . ?"

He put his hand on my shoulder and this time I didn't shake it off. He hesitated. "Lots of crazy thoughts go through my head. But they're not me. They're just thoughts that are passing through on their way to somewhere else. I just wave to them as they go by. 'Thank you for sharing.'"

José turned me to face him, so he could look straight into my eyes. "Listen to me,. Who I am, I'm not my thoughts. I'm just the person who has them for a while. I don't have to be them. And neither do you. Who you are, who I am—we're the people we choose to be. We chose this. You and I, we chose this together. You and I, Jamie. You and I."

I swallowed. "You sound like a trainer now."

"Well, yeah. Okay. Somebody had to stay awake during the boring parts. Otherwise they'd have sent us out running again."

I sniffled again, not as much this time. "I hear you," I said. "I just—I'm feeling overwhelmed."

"Yeah, me too. Let's be overwhelmed together." He pulled me close and we sat together for a while.

Feeling overwhelmed.

SIXTEEN

"It was an encoded message," Alec reported. "But not very reassuring."

We had gathered once again in the space that the North Station crew had set aside for us. This time, most of us were present, spaced around the walls and hanging from the overheads. Even a few members of the North Station crew.

"Morse code," he explained. "It's from hundreds of years ago, before we had real data transmission. It was one of the first uses of electricity, even before light bulbs. Oh, that's another one you'll have to look up. The way it worked, each of the twenty-six letters of the English alphabet were reduced to a specific set of dots and dashes and then the signal was transmitted through a direct wire connection. Dit-dit-dot-dot-dit-dit, and so on. And no, they didn't have radio signals yet. That came later. But morse code telegraphy worked well enough for a pre-digital era. It wasn't instantaneous, but a message could be sent across an entire continent in a matter of hours. That is, if weather and animals and other disruptions hadn't broken the line. And as long as you had operators repeating it at each station, sending it on."

"Thanks for the history lesson," called someone, a burly fellow named Johnson. "What did the message say?"

"I'm getting to that," said Alec. "What I want to point out is that whoever sent that signal intended it to be undetectable to anyone else up there, but just noticeable enough that someone down here would see it. The fluctuations were embedded into the least significant bit of the feedback signals that monitor synchronous engagement. That's information too. The context."

"Yes. But the message?" Johnson prompted.

Alec cleared his throat. "The signal decodes to three words. 'Don't come. Danger.' Then it repeats. Over and over again."

For a moment, no one said anything. Finally, the fellow next to Johnson grunted and raised his hand. Kovacs. Alec pointed to him.

"So the situation hasn't changed, has it?"

"No, it hasn't."

"Does downline know?"

"They're the ones who decoded it. One of the historians recognized the pattern of fluctuations."

"And what do they say we should do?"

"I was just getting to that." Alec took a deep breath. "Immigration Authorities have suggested several possibilities, but the most likely one, and

I tend to agree—there may have been some kind of a coup on Praxis. They've collated all the news that came out before the portal was closed, and it suggests that there was a very well-organized extremist faction. That faction apparently seized control of the station. Apparently. We don't know who's in charge, but whoever it is, they now have control of the entire supply chain, and if that's the case, then they have control of the entire Praxis colony."

"And what do they say we should do?" Kovacs repeated

"We could return," Alec said. "That's one option."

"And what about our contracts?"

Alec shook his head. "I don't know."

"We've been trained for Praxis. Is anyone else bidding on us?"

"Not that I know of."

"So it's the Labor Corps anyway, right?"

"I don't know. That hasn't been decided. Maybe, if Praxis reopens—maybe we could . . . I don't know." Alec looked unhappy.

"You could go back to training. The rest of us —"

For the first time, Alec lost his patience. "Do you think I'm happy about this? Goddammit! I hate this as much as you do! I know what we're all facing—and I'm in the middle. I get to pass all this information back and forth and I have no control over any of this! And goddammit again, you are so goddamn important to me, I don't want to let you down, I don't want to lose you!" And then he stopped himself in mid-outburst. He held up a hand, took several deep breaths, and regained a semblance of composure.

"There is another option. I don't know how I feel about it. It's dangerous. But Immigration Authority says we're on site, so—maybe there's something we could try. They told me to pass this thought to you to see what you think. Whatever you decide. It's your choice."

SEVENTEEN

Finally, Kovacs said, "You're talking some kind of military operation, aren't you?"

Alec nodded. "Yes."

Hanging on the wall next to him, Johnson said, "It's not really a choice, is it? This or the Labor Corps."

Alec shook his head. "That hasn't been decided."

"But it's on the table, isn't it?"

Alec shrugged. "I don't know."

"You don't know a lot."

"I only know what they're telling me, okay? I'm not hiding anything from you. Remember, I'm in this too."

Johnson scowled, but he didn't reply to that.

Kovacs said, "So what kind of military operation are they suggesting?"

Alec shook his head. "A couple dozen of you are ex-military. You know how to plan an operation. I don't. I can give you terrain maps, tunnel maps, schematics, power distribution and communication networks, and—"

"What about equipment?"

One of the North Station crew spoke up then, a young fellow named Mal. "We can probably fab some gear for you. Helmets, goggles, armor, and—"

"Weapons?"

Mal hesitated. After a moment, he nodded. "Yeah, we could do that too. We'd have to take one of the fabbers offline, take it out of the net so there's no record of what it's printing, but, yeah. We can do it."

Kovacs didn't look happy. He looked around the chamber, checking to see who was present. "All right," he said. "We'll talk it over." He looked around again, this time inviting. "Anyone over the rank of grunt, anyone with experience in logistics and planning." Back to Alec. "How soon can you provide maps?"

Alec nodded. "Well, you have the orientation material, you can start there. I'll have the rest assembled in an hour. Downline has some material you might want too, their assessment of what kind of equipment Praxis might have or might have been able to build. But we won't know how many or how well trained."

Kovacs said, "But if it's a coup, we won't be fighting the whole colony, just the fanatics." Then he said something scary, "I don't mind killing fanatics."

Alec stared across at him. "Just don't

71

become one yourself."

Kovacs grunted. "Not a problem. I intend to die in bed. Making love to a magnificent redhead."

"An Irish Setter?" asked Johnson and the whole room erupted in laughter.

EIGHTEEN

José and I did not volunteer to join Kovacs' Krushers. There were some thirty others who were far more qualified—and eager to go and do something serious. José observed they had a lot of emotional energy invested in hurting someone back. At least, this had the potential to be a positive action.

A lot of us sat in on their meetings and discussions, their planning sessions, and endless arguments over details. It was something to do, and once in a while, some of us were able to offer a useful thought.

But no meeting was complete until Kovacs turned to Alec and asked, "What do you think?"

To his credit, Alec did not try to second-guess any of their plans. "I don't have a military background," he would say. "You're the experts, so maybe my question is something you've already addressed, but I was wondering about . . ." And that would usually spark another thirty minutes of discussion, most of it useful. Alec was smart enough to give away leadership.

The bigger problem was equipment. Most of the cargo we were carrying to Praxis was agricultural, not a lot of it was industrial. So North Station had to pull two fabbers offline to generate the gear the assault team would need. Sometimes we saw the Krushers trying on armor or helmets, running tests on personal flyers, or just pondering designs on tablets or wall-displays.

A two-car cargo train arrived, not listed on any schedule, it carried things in ominous gray boxes. The assault team unloaded the cars quickly and they rolled back through the return portal as if they had never been here. After that, the only problem was the upline insertion.

The Krushers planned to split themselves into four separate assault teams. Each would embed themselves in the countryside long enough to determine their targets. They would communicate at randomly selected times, using splatter-coding to make their messages sound like static. Everyone was invited to consider obstacles and solutions, but it seemed like the Krushers were way ahead of us.

The one part that needed the most thought was how to get the assault teams through the portal to Praxis. The portal itself had to be kept open and operative. If it was completely shut down, there was no way to reopen it. But the enclosing airlocks were shuttered.

It was Mal from the North Station team

who suggested a way through. "Follow the power cables," he said. "The portals have to be kept in perfect equilibrium. Balanced on both sides. There's not a lot of wiggle room. If we were to ship mass back and forth, we'd be transferring the mass of every train, so we do it with power, automatically transmitting megawatts back every time any mass goes through. Available power limits the amount of mass that can go through at any time, that's why trains have to be short. There are special maintenance tunnels with their own airlocks just for the power transmission. I'll bet your coup plotters haven't realized that. Not yet anyway."

"But those locks have to be monitored, right?" That was Kovacs. "If we try to go through, they'll be alerted. Can we shut down the monitors?"

Mal shook his head. "That would set off alarms. No. But—" He repositioned himself on the wall, leaned forward intensely. "The cable airlocks run separate from the trains. What if they have very limited manpower? What if they're only guarding the tracks? And even if they are monitoring the cable locks, they might not have guards on them. The airlock guards would be half a klick away. So even if there are alarms, you would still have a chance to get in and go to ground."

"And . . ." said Johnson. "Think about this. They might not have their most experienced, most lethal guards at the airlocks. Maybe just some untrained buttons."

"Or maybe—" responded Kovacs, "they're not taking any chances, and have a team of gorillas there. We don't know." He turned back to Mal, nearly losing his grip on the wall handle. "You said half a klick. How's the gravity over there?"

"Nearly a gee. You're going to feel the difference. You're going to pay for every day in low-gee. You have to act soon."

Kovacs didn't look happy. "We'll have to chance it." He looked around the chamber. "Right. We're waiting for one more shipment from downline. With or without, we have to go." He glanced around at his team. "Listen up, use the gym, every moment you can. Stay in shape. You're no good to anyone falling down over there. Get pumped. Oh-six-hundred hours, we go."

NINETEEN

A nd then the whole plan fell apart.

Praxis sent a message. A very short message.

"The portal will open tomorrow at 1800 hours for fifteen minutes only, just long enough for a single pod to deliver . . ." followed by a list of supplies. "Do not send anything or anyone else."

Alec called the meeting, but Kovacs ran it. "The pod is ready. It's the supplies they were expecting. They probably need them more now than ever." He nodded to Mal who spent a few minutes discussing Praxis' import history and the importance of this cargo pad. Some of the cargo was industrial, some of it was utilitarian, a lot of it was packaged food stores, but quite a bit of it was luxuries—like pineapples and sodas, alcohol and cannabis. But there was also a field hospital and a large store of medical supplies and equipment. "Make of that what you will," he concluded.

Kovacs thanked him and looked around the chamber, up and down at all the men perched on the walls. "The core group has studied the situation, we do have options. None of them are great. Some of them might be better than others. We don't have a lot of time to make up our minds, so we need to keep the discussion short.

"First," he continued. "We could send the assault team in with the pod, ready to act as soon as it slides out of the airlock, but that's the obvious tactic and they'll expect us to try something like that—and it's an easy one to counter. They've had time to install barricades to keep any incursion immobilized. We could probably hold the pod, but we couldn't return because they control the airlocks. That'd be an ugly stalemate. They need their supplies, especially the field hospital, so we'd have something to trade, but there's no way to guarantee they'd let us return. That's not a winning situation, so it's off the table.

"Or . . ." Kovacs continued, "We can go in as we planned while their attention is on the pod. They'd still know we'd invaded, but unless they're smart enough to monitor the cable locks, we'd have a window of opportunity. We'd have enough time to fly out, over the hills and run a guerrilla operation from there. Before they could send in troops, we'd be several kilometers away."

He paused. "There is a danger to that one. If they have drones circling, or even aerial troops, they might be able to intercept. We have military-grade flyers, we don't know if they do. We have short range missiles, we don't know if they do. And we don't know what kind of detection gear they have. Our best bet is to keep close to the ground and stay lost in the noise. We've studied the maps, we have a good idea where we can go, but they have the home team advantage. So we're thinking of splitting into multiple small teams, each with its own mission. That's got a higher probability of success. That's our recommendation. Any questions?"

There were several, quickly dismissed. Kovacs' had assembled a good team. Their planning sessions had been thorough.

"There is another possibility," he said quietly. The room went silent. "What if we had a distraction? Something to keep them looking in the wrong place. If it bought us even an extra ten minutes, that could be the margin we need." He looked to Alec. "We need two volunteers to play a part. They'd ride in the pod with the supplies. Not military. Definitely not military. And definitely not part of our team. They'd be representatives of the Line Authority, arriving to evaluate the situation. Wanting an assessment of the situation. Needing to know if and when normal traffic could resume. Looking for certainty. Reassurances. Contracts. Treaties. All that stuff."

Kovacs looked around the chamber, looked at all the men hanging on the walls and the overhead. "We need, well . . . Rosencrantz and Guildenstern, two foolish young men, naïve and innocent and unaware that this is a dangerous

79

situation they've blundered into."

José and I looked at each other. "Uh-uh. No." We both said it at the same time.

TWENTY

Praxis has a weird orbit.

Not just weird. Unstable.

At some time in the past, maybe a few million years ago, something big collided with it and knocked the hell out of it, probably knocking it out of its previous orbit. It probably wobbled around its star for a few million years before falling into an elliptical orbit, except that orbit wasn't stable either. The star was in the center of the ellipse. For the orbit to be stable, the star would have to be off center. Praxis was working its way toward a more stable orbit, but at the moment, it was an anomaly with strange seasons and violent weather.

But for that reason, it was an astrophysicist's wet dream.

And yes, there was a sizable colony of researchers established there, with observatories and satellites studying how the system worked. Those men would probably be our most likely allies.

José and I went back to our cabin and vehemently agreed with each other. There was no-fucking-way that we would volunteer to be Kovacs' necessary distraction. Hell no to the max. Absolutely not. Don't even ask.

There was a knock on the cabin door. We both said, "Don't answer it," at the same time.

We answered it.

Alec and Kovacs floated outside. Sometimes people forgot to use their grip shoes. "Can we come in?"

"Before you ask, the answer is no," said José.

They looked at each other. Alec said, "You're not our first choice. But Hunter and Tyler can't do it."

José snorted. "All talk, no walk?"

"No," said Alec. "Tyler broke his arm."

"Huh?"

"Low-gee acrobatics. He didn't stick the landing."

José grunted. "Oh. Sorry to hear that. But the answer is still no."

"I don't like it either," said Kovacs. "But there isn't anybody else."

"I don't believe you. There's a hundred and thirty of us on this trip. Certainly—"

"It's not that," he said. "It's believability. You guys look the part."

"More than that," said Alec. "You act the part."

Kovacs sighed. "Look, if you're really that

afraid—"

"We're not afraid," I said. "And we're not cowards. It's just that—we're not actors. And there are better men on the team."

"We don't have a lot of time," said Alec. He looked to Kovacs. "Let's talk to Matthew."

Kovacs nodded. He pushed himself down to the floor, so his grip shoes could grab the carpet. He turned back to us. "The things is, a lot depends on the distraction. A lot of lives might be at risk. My life. The team's lives. Your teammates from the training." He looked to me. "You gave a great speech back there, about teams, about contribution, about doing what's necessary. That's why we thought of you. But, okay—"

"Shit," I said. "Yeah."

José looked to me. "Yeah," he agreed.

Alec looked to Kovacs. "Told you."

Kovacs ignored him, he looked to us. "We have three and a half hours," he said. "The station team will train you. Just get the lingo right, you'll do fine."

TWENTY-ONE

I n the movies, the heroes always know what to do.

In real life, nobody does anything without training and preparation. The movies always leave that part out. Or they tell you that all the training happened before the movie started.

We had two and a half hours of frenzied instructions, we had barely enough time to dress the part and meet at the pod. There were handshakes all around and even a few hugs. Kovacs' team came floating and bouncing past. They nodded in mutual recognition, offered a few quick words of encouragement, then disappeared into the pod.

We had three stations to go before we arrived at Praxis. All the locks between here and there were synchronized so we could go straight through.

Alec grabbed us both, more to keep us from floating away than to hug us, but the feeling was there anyway. "You guys are heroes," he said.

"Never doubt that."

"I'm not a hero," I said. "Maybe José is. He married me. But we're just doing what we have to do."

Alec looked at me hard. "Yes, that's what heroes do. They do what's in front of them. You're heroes."

I shrugged. Hard to do in low-gee without bouncing away, but I did it anyway. "Okay, fine."

José looked to Alec. "Any last instructions? Anything you forgot to tell us?"

Alec grinned. "Yeah. Don't screw it up. Now get on the pod and get out of here."

Once inside, we gathered in the lounge for coffee and final instructions from Kovacs.

"All right, first things first. Pee and poop. All of you. We'll hit gravity as soon as we move. You'll need to empty yourselves. You don't wanna do that on Praxis. We'll have more important things to do.

"Second," he continued. "This is a one-way trip. You knew that when we started, but this is it. We go to Praxis, whatever happens, we're not coming back. The quarantine stays in effect. But if we do our jobs right, everybody else will follow us.

"Third, this train isn't going to stop, but it will slow down before entering the final airlock. That's where the assault team rolls out. Once you're on the other side, we expect that they're going to halt the pod and scan it for heat signatures before letting it through." Kovacs looked to me and José. "They're going to be angry when they see you, but they'll see you're unarmed and they want their supplies, they'll let you through.

"We're hoping that they'll argue among themselves. The longer they argue, the more time the assault team has. But if they take too long, you know what to do. Send a message, 'What's the holdup? What's taking so long?' They'll let you through if only to demand an explanation.

"Here's the thing," Kovacs said. "We're not sure who the good guys are in this squabble."

He lifted his hands, a gesture that said everything and nothing. "We don't know. What if the bad actors are the ones calling for help? What if the good guys are the ones trying to maintain order? We just don't know." He turned to José and me. "That'll be your job. My teams are going to ground, hiding in the hills, scouting targets, but we'll be waiting for your signal to act. Red or Blue. That's all you have to send. Red for the bad actors, blue for the good. Take your time. Make sure of your assessment."

José nodded. "Got it." Kovacs looked to me. I nodded too.

The pod lurched. We were on our way.

TWENTY-TWO

We strapped ourselves in, Kovacs' orders. After Tyler's accident, nobody was taking chances. Every portal opened onto a different world, a different gravity, and a stomach-lurching transition. We alternately sagged in our seats, or felt like we were about to bounce out of them.

Some people might think that's fun. I didn't.

We rode for hours. The inbound and outbound portals had to be spaced far enough apart to avoid what the engineers called "interference." So most of the trip was the journey between portals. The screens that we had instead of windows showed us the landscapes of the worlds we were passing through. We didn't pay them much attention, Kovacs insisted on reviewing our briefings, quizzing us on what we might expect and how we should react.

For José and I, our roles were obvious. Play dumb. Be innocent. We don't know what's going on. We just know that traffic was interrupted. We were sent upline to determine if the situation is stable and how soon traffic can resume.

Of course, that pretense also suggested that we would be sending a report downline. Whoever was controlling Praxis would also want to control that information. That could be . . . risky.

But on the other hand, if there really was another hand, Praxis wasn't self-sufficient yet. They depended on the economic goodwill of the downline worlds. They needed to reestablish credibility, so maybe they would . . .

That was where we ran out of possibilities. All we had left was speculation.

The train ride was going to take a while. José and I went aft, found an empty cabin, and curled up together.

"You scared?"

"No more than usual."

"That much?"

"I married you anyway, didn't I?"

He smiled. "And I, you."

"Do you ever regret it?"

He thought about it. "No. You?"

I thought about it too. "No."

"Okay, then we're good."

"Let's get some sleep."

"If we can. Yes."

We wrapped ourselves around each other and drifted off. We woke up when the gravity changed, we were heavier now. We shifted position, spooning now, then rifted back to sleep.

We woke up again at the next transition.

One more transit. Just enough time to pee and poop and wash our faces.

Praxis lay ahead.

TWENTY-THREE

T he thing about laws—they aren't what we
think.

They're not rules.

They're agreements.

This is what we agree to so our community
can work.

The problem is that lawbreakers don't agree.
Obviously.

We learn it in school as soon as we're
old enough to understand the concept of an
agreement. Well, we're supposed to learn it.

And we have to honor those agreements,
because we promised to.

Lawbreakers don't.

And that's the problem.

Lawbreakers see the rest of us as weak,
bound by our agreements. They see the
agreements as uncomfortable rules, as limits, as
an oppressing authority defining what they can
and can't do. They see themselves as stronger than
the rest of us because they aren't limited by the

rules, the laws, the agreements.

That's the short version.

So how do lawful people protect themselves against lawbreakers without breaking their own agreements to the community—their own laws? José said it to me after that battle in the training barracks. "If we're the good guys, we have to act like it. Everywhere. The difference between us and them, we can't become them. That's gotta be our way."

In theory, that sounds good. In practice, it's . . . always a test.

If we had known that, realized it, lived it before that stupid soccer riot—yeah, it was a riot— we might still be students at the university, might still be in our own little bubbles of selfishness, indifference, and alienation, we wouldn't be married, and wouldn't be on our way to Praxis.

We wouldn't be here.

But we were.

So . . . we had to be the good guys. Everywhere.

But especially here.

Because here was where we were going to spend the rest of our lives.

The pod slowed down, we were approaching the final airlock, the last transition before Praxis. We entered the first tunnel. Kovacs' men were already stationed inside the pods' airlocks. We felt the hatches pop and a moment later, we felt them thudding shut again. The assault team had rolled out into darkness.

José and I were alone in the car.

"Let's sit down," he said. "Gravity."

"Yeah."

We sat. We buckled in.

We went through the first airlock chamber, the doors slid shut behind us as we rolled into the transfer chamber. The portal glimmered ahead. We could see through it to the other side—we rolled through.

The shift to Praxis' gravity wasn't rough. We were going from 77% to 89.3%, somewhere in the southern temperate zone. It felt like a bump.

The next doors slammed shut behind the pod and we were in the final airlock.

Praxis.

According to their instructions, the pod would be held in the final airlock while they scanned it for contraband.

Us.

"Well," said José. "We're here." He looked at me sharply. "Jamie? We're gonna be okay." He reached over and squeezed my hand.

I hoped he was right.

TWENTY-FOUR

T he pod stopped.

    We looked to the screens that served as windows.

We saw a line of men in black armor, faceless helmets, and serious-looking weapons. All of them were studying at the pod—as if they could see us. They were behind a wall of glass. One more protection against infection. Theirs and ours.

Behind the armored men, several others were sitting at semi-circular consoles. They wore featureless white jumpsuits. They studied the screens in front of them, monitoring all their separate scans.

They conferred. No contraband in the pod.

Except us, of course.

One of them looked up at the pod. The team leader? Probably. He was a tall man, burly, with shaggy dark hair that fell to his shoulders. He spoke as an authority. "We sent very clear instructions. The pod was to be unmanned. No passengers."

José turned on the camera. We held up our newly minted credentials. "We're not immigrants. We are legal agents of the Line Authority and this is a formal investigation. I am Agent James Patrick Dolan and this is Agent José Michael Rodríguez-Chan. We are here to determine the interruption of line service and expedite the resumption of traffic."

The man was unconvinced. "Praxis is closed."

"Please identify yourself," said José.

"Franklin Yoh, Acting Coordinator. Praxis is closed."

"Thank you, Coordinator Yoh. Please make arrangements for our inspection tour."

"That's not possible. Praxis is a quarantine world. You won't be able to return."

"We have multi-zone bio-suits. We have a decontamination unit at North Station."

Yoh shook his head. "Not acceptable." He conferred with his associates. "You will not leave the pod. You will offload your cargo and return to wherever you came from."

José shook his head. "No. Not acceptable. If you won't allow inspection, we won't offload cargo."

Yoh did not look happy. "Apparently, we have a stalemate."

"So it seems."

"Praxis is closed," Yoh repeated. "There are no inhabited worlds upline, only a few exploratory stations."

"It is the well-being of those stations that we are concerned with, as well as the astrophysicists at the Praxis observatory, and the researchers at six other stations."

Yoh didn't have an immediate answer for that. He switched off his microphone and gathered his associates into a hasty conference. They kept their backs to us to avoid any lip-reading software we might have.

José switched off our microphones and turned me away from our cameras. "They haven't tried using force."

"Yet," I said.

"He did give us his name. That's a good sign."

"Maybe. Or maybe he just wants us to know who to fear."

"They really want our supplies—"

"Not badly enough. Not yet."

We turned back to the screen. Yoh and his team were still arguing among themselves. Finally, they faced us again. "Praxis is closed," Yoh repeated.

"Is that your final position?" asked José.

"It is," said Yoh.

José straightened. "You give us no choice. We will return this pod to North Station. When the legally authorized representatives of Praxis Station are ready to negotiate, you will send a formal note of compliance, with full notarization. Until then, no traffic of any kind will be coming upline, and no contact will be initiated until all negotiations are concluded." He turned to me. "Prepare for return."

I picked up my tablet and pretended to study it. I turned to José. "Ready to engage. Whenever you order."

José turned back to the screen. "Do you wish to confer with your associates again?"

"We've made our decision."

"So be it," said José. He was serious. He took a deep breath and turned to me—

"Wait!"

That was a member of Yoh's team. Almost frantically, he pulled the Coordinator aside. We couldn't understand what he said, it was in another language, but his tone was urgent. The two of them turned their backs to us. The others gathered around them. This time the argument was visibly more heated.

José and I turned away from the camera. "They need the field hospital."

I agreed. "That suggests serious injuries."

"Maybe."

We turned back just as Yoh faced forward. He did not look happy. "We will allow a limited inspection. Under our supervision."

"Unacceptable," said José. "The Line Authority has authorized us to inspect everything that might affect the resumption of traffic. We cannot accept any restrictions."

Another conference by Yoh and his

associates.

José and I turned away again. "Is this how formal negotiations work?"

"I don't know. It all seems a little desperate to me."

"On which side?"

"Both, I think."

TWENTY-FIVE

A pop and a woosh and our airlock door slid open. The sound was filtered through the earpieces of our bio-suits.

José and I stood on the platform waiting for Coordinator Yoh to open the glass partition. Our harness cameras recorded everything, picture, sound, position, temperature, air pressure, atmosphere, and several other things that had not been explained. Coordinator Yoh and his team wore similar devices. Fair enough. Ours was being beamed back to North Station. We didn't know who was monitoring theirs.

We had maps on our helmet displays. Humans had settled mostly in the southern hemisphere of the planet, most of the research stations were located there as well as the three largest communities. This war partly due to the accessibility of the southern continents, but also because the night sky was far more interesting in the south, presenting some astonishing views of the local galaxy. Galaxies, like star systems, have livability zones, where conditions are better suited for life. Praxis was on the inner edge.

Like the other shirtsleeve worlds, Praxis had dual citizenship—those who had gone native and exposed themselves to the native life, and those who wanted someday to return downline, they lived in separate sealed environments. It they needed to go out and take samples for study, they wore multi-layered bio suits, like we were wearing. They went in and out through triple airlocks. They returned to their sealed environments through aggressive decontamination procedures. And hoped that would be enough.

The local joke about Praxis is that its weird magnetic field also works on scientists. At least half of the researchers who come to Praxis, planning to avoid exposure to native life, working only in sealed environments, find the challenges so exciting, they choose to go native. They join the shirtsleeve community. They'll spend the rest of their lives discovering the marvelous intricacies of this new world.

That's what José and I had signed up for, we hadn't planned on investigating a coup, but here we were, officially deputized representatives of the downline authority. As investigators, we were required to wear bio-suits and go through multiple airlocks and decontamination chambers everywhere.

Our first stop was the research station thirty klicks north. Two of Yoh's aides drove us there in a cargo pod that had been turned into a dual-environment bus. Privately, we called them Frick and Frack, or Mutt and Jeff, or Statler and Waldorf. We assumed they were listening, probably recording, but they never said anything. They had been trained to be perfect little robots.

The accommodations weren't bad. The bottom half of the bus was for permanent residents of Praxis, the top half, where we rode, was a sealed environment for temporary residents —installation teams, inspection agencies, Line authorities, and the occasional representatives of the Covenant of Human Rights.

We bounced along a roughly carved dirt road that had been battered by weather. The station was a rough assemblage of cargo pods and tunnels, studded with antennas. We passed through the inevitable airlocks, and got bio-scanned anyway for microbial contaminations Our unsuited driver did not accompany us. He didn't want to suit up just to enter the station, he'd wait in the bus.

Once inside, we were greeted by Frederik Ederman, Head of Station, and several other scraggly men who had apparently been too busy to bathe any time recently. I assumed they were busy because the station didn't seem to be having any problems with their water recycling units, and they were visibly annoyed at this interruption of their work.

Because it was still daylight, the rest of the

station's staff were either sleeping or too engaged in studying the previous evening's observations. Apparently, there had been a spectacular supernova in this stellar neighborhood recently. But those who did greet us were eager to share the most interesting of the oddities they had discovered.

After a quick tour of the station, we gathered in the lounge for tea and biscuits. "We have a theory," Ederman said with visible enthusiasm. "It's probably wrong, but there's enough circumstantial evidence that we can argue it both ways. What if this portal opens to a time more than four million years into our future? What if Praxis circles a star in the Andromeda galaxy and when night falls, you can see the Milky Way galaxy dominating the sky? it's less than a light year away and we're on a collision course. Okay, we think it's the Milky Way, it kinda matches, but maybe it isn't. There are a trillion unmapped galaxies in our time. But anyway, here on Praxis, we have box seats for an imminent galactic collision. It'll happen another five hundred thousand years, that's when the gravitational effects start pulling both galaxies apart. Oh, do you have any news of our request for a launch system? We really need to put some big scopes into orbit."

"Sorry," José said. "That's very exciting and we wish we had time to hear more, but unfortunately, we're only here to assess the political situation. Can you tell us anything about that?"

Ederman looked confused. "Um, no. Sorry. I'm sure the local situation is interesting, but in here, we're mostly looking skyward. Maybe the geologists, or whatever they call themselves. Praxologists? We have had some supply interruptions recent, nothing serious, I'm sure whatever it is, it'll be sorted out soon. It's not a problem, we have a farm, we grow most of our own vegetables, but we do import a lot of things we don't grow. Mostly protein, beer, wine, sodas, chocolate, coffee, data-dumps, especially data-dumps. There's been some remarkable observations being made on some of the transit stations . . ."

He went on like that for a while. After a bit José and I looked to each other. We shared a nod of agreement.

"Thank you for your hospitality," I said. "We'll certainly send a note downline supporting your request for a launch system and the personnel to run it. But as my colleague pointed out, there are too many requests of all kinds, and there's a shortage of qualified personnel to assemble and run such an installation, especially in almost one-gee environment like Praxis."

Ederman led us back to the docking tunnel that connected to our bus and we made our way through the multiple airlocks. Once we were on our way again, I sighed. "I don't know if they're lucky or foolish. They have no idea."

"I think they're both," said José. "They're lucky to have a challenge that they love. And if they're foolish, maybe it's the right kind of foolish. I almost envy them. Almost." He reached over and squeezed my hand.

TWENTY-SIX

The Praxology Station was a little more down to earth. That's the way they explained it. Pun intended.

They had dug bore holes as deep into the planet's core as their equipment would go, and like the astrophysicists, they were eager to share everything they had discovered.

I don't know about José, but what's under the crust of a planet is not high on my list of things I need to know about. But the Praxologists were just as excited to share their discoveries as the astrophysicists. They assumed José and I were specifically interested.

We came away knowing that Praxis has a scattering of useful metals—iron, aluminum, copper, tin, nickel, zinc, even some silver and gold —not as much as could be found elsewhere or mined as easily, and certainly not as cost effective as importing raw metals from industrial sites on asteroids and transition stations. But the presence of these metals did explain a lot about Praxis' origin and history.

The Praxologists didn't have much to say about the political situation either. They did admit to an interruption in supplies, but nothing critical, they were okay for now. Would you like to tour the bore hole? Maybe later, thanks.

José and I spent the night in the pod, while our driver headed to our next destination. We held each other close and whispered together. "I think they're sending us everywhere but where we need to go."

I agreed. "Tomorrow, Dersham Station." The closest thing to a real city on Praxis.

José nodded. "Let's get some sleep." He kissed me goodnight and rolled over. I didn't know what to feel. Getting my emotions turned back on gave me too many uncomfortable moments. I didn't know how I was supposed to feel about anything. I lay awake for a while wondering about everything until finally I drifted asleep with nothing resolved.

It was still dark when we woke. Frick was driving now, Frack was probably sleeping, but we were still a long way from anywhere. I fixed a light meal in the galley, coffee with cream and sugar, eggs over easy, maple bacon, cheddar cheese, croissants, jam or salsa, butter, salt and pepper. Nothing fancy, just sufficient for the moment. Some of it was imported, some of it was produced here. I don't claim to be a great cook, but so far nobody has died at the table. José pronounced it satisfactory and that was enough.

"It makes good sense to feed us well," he said. "It puts us in a better mood. We're more likely to say they were good hosts."

"So were the—" I stopped myself before I made the comparison. "Never mind."

José smiled at my self-interruption. "I read somewhere that after you get your feelings restarted that you could have some trouble with impulse control. But you seem to be doing okay."

"I'm feeling it," I said. "I mean, a lot of it is nice. You are. Mostly. But some of it is uncomfortable. Scary. I'll figure it out. I think. I hope."

"It takes time," José said. "I can be patient."

"What about you? I mean, you got recalibrated. How does that work?"

He frowned, thinking about it. "It's like— like they said. It's like discovering a new room in your house. It's a nice room, but parts of it are unfamiliar. Strange. But so far . . ." He nodded. "Yeah, it's a nice room. Okay?"

"Okay."

We sat in silence for a while, drinking our coffee and finishing our meal. We'd been married for three months and already I was wondering if this was how marriage would be all the time, always a little uncertain—or did it ever settle into a comfortable routine?

I wouldn't know until it did.

TWENTY-SEVEN

Frick and Frack, or Mutt and Jeff, or Statler and Waldorf, depending on our mood, did not argue with us when we told them we wanted to go directly to Dersham. They swung the bus into a new heading and we bounced west across the landscape.

When the blue glare of the sun finally crept up over the horizon behind us, brown shadows stretched across the land ahead of us. As the day slowly brightened we got our first look at this strange, amazing landscape. The displays that served as windows revealed a rolling panorama.

Strong winds had swept across this plain for centuries, shaping the land, the rocks, the trees. The rocks were polished on their windward side and the trees were permanently bent and curled. Their leaves were red and brown and yellow—chlorophyll hadn't evolved here, instead the different ecology of Praxis had given rise to another mechanism for using sunlight to turn CO_2 into growth.

In the distance, we could see a herd of animals, we assumed they were animals. They were the size of blimps and covered with long yellow hair that stretched out behind them in the wind. They were all turned into it with their heads down. They were feeding on the high pink grass that covered these hills. The grass leaned away from the ever-present wind. Occasionally the bus rocked from the force of it.

"Interesting weather," said José.

I grunted agreement. The coffee hadn't finished brewing yet.

Another display showed we were less than an hour out of Dersham station. It was on the other side of the hills in front of us, set deep inside a sheltering crater.

José grabbed his mug and sat down at the desk. He logged in and began sending messages to possible contacts at Dersham. He had the list of people we needed to talk to.

Almost immediately, the mail came bouncing back. "This contact is not available." And even more ominously, "This contact is no longer available."

"Coordinator Yoh must have called ahead."

José nodded and sipped at his own coffee. "Let's just do our job. As best as we can." He specifically did not mention the details. We were intended as a distraction. Our sole responsibility was to signal Red, White, or Blue. Red would trigger an assault on the coup. Blue would trigger an assault on a tyrannical authority. White . . . ? Both sides were culpable, seize the portal and hold it until the Line Authority could install a protectorate.

And if anything happened to us and we were unable to send any signal at all, Kovacs' teams would implement the white option.

I sipped at my coffee. It wasn't great, but it was drinkable. "Maybe we'll get a better breakfast at Dersham."

José swiveled to look at me. "Breakfast," he said. "That will be a very important signal. If they treat us well, that will mean one thing. If they treat us badly, that will mean something else. And if they treat us very well, we'll need to be suspicious."

Dersham was an assortment of odd-shaped structures, mostly adapted cargo pods, but also a few domes, piles of shipping containers, antennas, scopes, and a few towers for generating electricity, and others for sucking water out of the atmosphere. The unending winds kept Dersham's lights on and the toilets flushing.

We put on our bio-suits and passed through several airlocks until we arrived at a converted pod that was used as a holding facility for temps. Breakfast was delivered through a one-way tube. Disposable plates and utensils. It wasn't a feast, but it wasn't awful either. We were served several kinds of fruit, some unidentifiable sweet green melon, several kinds of cheese, bacon-infused omelets, thick slices of ham-like protein, blueberry muffins, and a few things that were probably imported, butter, peach jam, and somewhat better coffee.

A nameless assistant told us that our first appointment wouldn't be available until midshift, so we showered and napped and waited.

Nobody showed up at midshift. They sent in lunch, but gave us no updates about who or when. Nobody showed up at endshift either. It was only high noon on Praxis, the days were nearly 40 hours long. The endshift meal was sandwiches and something that might have been beer, but made from carrots or potatoes or some other root vegetable. Turnips perhaps?

I said to José, "This is deliberate, isn't it?"

"Probably. Either that or no one wants to talk to us."

"You think they're afraid?"

"Or in prison."

"Or . . ."

"Yeah," he agreed.

Neither one of us said anything for a while.

TWENTY-EIGHT

Finally, I said, "I think I'm tired of waiting. No, I'm tired of being treated rudely. Let's talk about Plan B."

José raised an eyebrow. He could do that. I couldn't. I'd practiced in front of the mirror. I could frown, but I couldn't raise an eyebrow. I think it's a skill. "Plan B?" he said. "Okay. When?"

I took a deep breath. "What I've seen of Praxis, so far? I'm not impressed. It does not match any of the pictures we saw back home."

"We've only seen a small part of the planet. The ugly windy part." He pointed to a map display. "Supposedly, there are more hospitable places."

I grunted. "Well, so far, calling this a 'shirtsleeve world' is a very generous description."

José didn't argue with that. "You're in a bad mood, aren't you?"

"I'm impatient."

"Yes, that's one of your more endearing traits."

I gave him the look. He gave it back to me.

We both started laughing. We refilled our coffee mugs and thought about what to do next.

José suggested, "Perhaps we should let Coordinator Yoh know that we are . . . um, annoyed."

I said, "Impatient."

He nodded and turned to the keyboard, speaking aloud as he typed. "Coordinator Yoh, are we to assume that this failure to provide information is a deliberate non-cooperation? Please let us know what your intentions are. Our agency needs specific information and if we cannot provide that, then Line Authority will have no choice but to take unilateral action. Please advise as soon as possible. Let me note that we already overdue to file today's report. We do not want to report deliberate non-cooperation. Please advise as to the delay in moving forward."

José looked to me. "Is that strong enough?"

I thought for a moment. "No. I think we made ourselves clear at the portal station. Can you put some teeth into it?"

Now it was his turn to think. José usually had the better communication skills. I had to think about what I wanted to say before I said it—or as José put it, I had to stew for a while, while my thoughts boiled and bubbled to the surface of my internal cauldron. Ha ha, very funny, but he was right. I needed to think. So if he said he had to think about something, he needed to be certain he was saying it clearly.

"Okay, try this." He turned back to the keyboard. I looked over his shoulder and read the words on the screen. "We are required to file a report every twelve hours, Earth time. If we fail to file three consecutive reports, Line Authority will have no choice but to stop all supply shipments until full cooperation is again restored. Your immediate response is required. You have six hours."

"Yeah, that works. Send it."

He nodded, reread it carefully, corrected one phrase, nodded again in satisfaction, and sent it.

"Okay. We just lit the fuse. Let's wait for the bang."

We waited. A long time. By the time code on the messages, it was eight hours before Yoh replied, and his note was succinct. "Message received. We will arrange a meeting shortly."

We looked at each other, puzzled.

Now, I don't mind looking at José. He's not hard to look at. And maybe it's me and maybe it's the rechanneling and maybe it was just that we were spending a different kind of time together, our relationship was changing, deepening, special —but I was starting to find him attractive in a way I hadn't noticed before.

So, I didn't mind the wait. It would be more alone time.

"Okay," I said.

"Yep," he agreed.

TWENTY-NINE

Fourteen hours later, the email chimed. José raised himself up on one elbow and looked at me. We'd made good use of the time. Excellent use. No regrets.

I almost didn't want to get out of bed. But I rolled out anyway and went to the desk. José followed. He reached past me to access the note. It was from Coordinator Yoh. "We have scheduled a meeting for thirteen o'clock. Be at your access port an hour before that. A bus will pick you up."

"That's it?" I asked.

"That's it."

"That's not very informative."

José didn't answer. He was thinking. He sat down and faced the screen. He studied the note for a moment, as if by rereading it he could determine what was behind it, what it really meant. He leaned back in his chair.

"What do you think?"

"I don't know," he said. Then, after a bit, he added, "I think they're still jerking us around." He fell silent.

I guessed he was having one of his quiet thoughtful moods. Usually, I left him alone until he was ready to talk. Or play. Or just get back to work. Or anything. He finally got up and went to the coffee machine. He looked over to me. "You want coffee?"

I nodded.

He fiddled with the machine for a while. He said, without looking up, "You've been . . . quiet for a while. What are you worrying about?"

"Nothing," I lied.

"Jamie," he said. "I can hear the gears grinding."

"I'm fine."

He looked over at me. "Whatever it is, tell me now, before it festers and turns into something serious."

"It's nothing." I hesitated. "It's just me being stupid, okay?"

"Sorry, no. I don't marry stupid people."

"How many people have you married?"

"Stop trying to change the subject."

He turned back to the coffee machine, waiting for the cups to fill. I could tell he was hurt. Or annoyed with me.

I cleared my throat. "Um, there is something."

He looked at me.

"Um, this isn't easy."

He sat down opposite me. He reached across

and took my hand. "Okay, forget coffee. What?"

I hesitated. "Um . . . do you ever regret—"

José frowned at me. It took him a moment to fill in the blanks. He shook his head. "Of course not. Not anymore."

"I mean, maybe before, you know, the changes—?"

"Ummm . . ." He paused, thinking back. "Okay, yes, I had thoughts. Misgivings. Feelings. But by then . . ." He shrugged. "I figured we had to go all the way and it would be all right. They said it would be." He shrugged. "And I trusted them. I trusted the evidence. So yeah, I did. And then we did. And it's turned out okay. Okay?"

"Okay," I said. "But I think I'm asking the wrong question."

He waited while I figured out how to approach the subject. From the top or the bottom or the north or the south, from the outside working my way toward the kernel of understanding—there was just no way but to ask. "Did you do it with women? A lot?"

"Only one. Two. Okay, three. But those last two were flings, not relationships."

"Um . . ."

"You want to know how this compares, don't you? You want to know if I'm happy. Am I right?"

I nodded.

José took a breath before answering. "Yes, I am. Very."

"Really?"

"Really."

"Okay. That's all I wanted to know."

He shook his head. "No. What you really want to know is there a difference? And if it's better."

I nodded again, reluctantly.

He got up and fetched the coffee. He put the mug down in front of me and waited till I had taken my first sip.

"Okay, look," he said. "First, you're an idiot. We're here. We're on Praxis. We're married. And we do it. A lot. Because it's fun. That should be enough for most people. But not for you, because you like to overthink everything. But that's okay too because it's part of who you are. So I'm going to explain it to you, and I want you to hear me, really hear me."

I swallowed and nodded. "Okay, yes."

José took both my hands in his again. "It's this simple. She was fun. A lot of fun. We were good together. But it didn't last, because maybe we weren't good enough to last. You—being with you, it's intense. In every way, but yes, in the best way too. I don't know if that's me or the rechanneling or whatever. But it's the way I'm experiencing it. It's intense. And I like it. But there's something else, something you need to know, even more than that."

I waited. He gathered his thoughts.

"Sex isn't about the physical," he said. "I

117

mean, it is. But that's not all it is. Maybe it is for some people. Maybe it's their only way of escaping their bodies for a moment. But for people who actually love each other—like you and me—sex is about the connection, the you and me part of it. No, wait—" He paused to consider his next words.

"Those moments when we're moving together, synchronized in pleasure, each of us being part of the same larger experience, something that connects us into something bigger than both of us, something that gets us out of our heads and into some other space that's so far removed from all the stuff we think we are and transforms us into . . . I don't know how to say it, I don't think there are words, but it's not just the physical, Jamie, it's something else, something more than that—that's an intensity I've never had before. Maybe it's the rechanneling. Maybe it's me. Maybe it's something I'm finally letting myself have, but I'm not giving it up. I'm here with you and there isn't anything or anyone or anything I can imagine that would make me give you up. Does that answer your question?"

I sniffled. I wiped my nose on my sleeve. José handed me a tissue. I wiped my eyes. I gulped hard. I finally found some words, but I never got to say them because he grabbed me and kissed me. A lot. For a long time.

And I relaxed. We were finally complete.

THIRTY

We put on our bio-suits, just in case.

We went through the airlocks and climbed into the bus.

There was no coffee. There were no muffins, no bread, no cheese, nothing. The pantry was empty. The cooler was empty. The pod had been stripped bare. Even the seat cushions were gone.

Like a prison.

"Well, that answers that question."

"I don't think it was ever a question," said José. "They're just letting us know. The pretense is over."

I didn't answer that. The pod bumped forward. The displays that served as windows were blanked and dead, so we had no idea where we were or where we were going.

I wanted to scratch my ear, but my bio-suit prevented that. I switched to the common channel and hoped that only José could hear me. I doubted that though. They had to be monitoring our every communication.

I looked across at José. His expression was hard to see behind the face mask. "We haven't seen much here, have we?"

"Uh-uh."

"Do you think Praxis is self-sufficient enough to survive without supplies from the Line Authority?"

José shook his head.

"Maybe they know something we don't?"

"They must think they do."

I had to ask. "Even so . . . why the sudden change?" I gestured around. "This doesn't make sense. I mean, wouldn't they want to look like they're cooperating?"

"Unless . . . I don't know." He got serious. "Let's not speculate. We don't want to say anything we don't want them to hear."

I nodded. "Right." Then, I added, "Can I say they're acting like assholes?"

I could hear the smile in his voice. "Yeah, you can say that."

We didn't have far to go.

The bus came to a stop and after a while, we heard and felt the connection tube linking up to the pod's airlock. The hatch opened automatically, an invitation.

We made our way through to a featureless chamber. The opposite wall was glass. On our side, there were benches. And on the benches—twelve members of Kovacs' team. But not Kovacs. I recognized two squad leaders, Anjin and Morne.

None of the men were wearing bio-suits. This was a sealed room.

One of them scratched his nose casually, but he looked directly at us, one finger still vertical, still touching his nose, but across his lips. A don't-say-anything gesture. Uh-huh, I made no sign of recognition. I continued looking around the room.

José said, "I guess we can strip off the suits."

"Yeah. My ears itch."

We went off to a corner and helped each other out of our gear. José looked at me intensely. "I don't know any of these guys," he lied. "Do you?"

I got his meaning immediately. I shook my head. "Strangers to me."

José nodded in silent approval. He finished pulling off his suit and helped me with mine. He grabbed my hand and held it for a moment. Reassurance. Then we went and sat down on the far end of one of the benches, as far as we could get from the men we said we didn't know.

We waited in silence. I reached over and laid my hand on top of José's. He waited a moment, then pulled away. I understood. Let's not give them any more information than they needed. Unless, of course, they'd recorded everything we'd said since we'd arrived.

After a long while, Coordinator Yoh entered the room on the other side of the glass. He looked to José and me. "You can stop pretending. We know you know these men. We know they came through at the same time you did. We know they came through the power exchange tunnels. And we know there are eighteen more. We expect to have them in custody shortly."

He paused, then as if he was remembering something else, he added, "And we know you two are phonies, not representatives of the Line Authority at all. And no, I will not be taking questions. This communication is one way. Your microphones are not turned on and whatever you might say, I won't be able to hear you. When the court convenes, then you will have a chance to speak. But so far, we can't find a lawyer who's willing to take your case."

He turned and left.

I put my arm around José's shoulders and pulled him close so I could whisper directly into his ear. "Don't cry. Don't give them that." Then I pulled him into a hug, so he could discreetly wipe his nose on my shirt.

THIRTY-ONE

T he lawyer's name was Hassan O'Larsen, and he did not look happy.

He came in carrying three tablets, followed by a young dark-featured assistant carrying two more. O'Larsen faced forward and the lights in the room came up. He looked at all of us, sighed, nodded, and turned to his assistant. "Turn on their microphones."

Back to us again, he studied us for a moment, cleared his throat and began. "Yes, I represent all of you. The whole group. And no, I did not volunteer. I was assigned. Against my will. But . . ." He sighed. "I will represent you to the best of my ability. Because . . . I dunno. Why not?"

José and I looked at each other. "Really?"

Several of the other men on the benches were already standing, all starting to talk at once, making demands, asking questions, a cacophony of confusion.

José grunted in annoyance. He stood up and went to the front of the glass. I followed. José waved the other men down before he turned back to O'Larsen.

"I'll speak for us," José said. "What are we charged with?"

"Nothing yet. They're still deciding."

"Who's they?"

"Coordinator Yoh and the Justice Committee."

"The Justice Committee?"

O'Larsen shrugged. "They were just convened. We don't normally have courts or lawyers."

"You're a lawyer?"

"I was. Back on Earth. Thought I was done with it."

"Well, here we are, aren't we?" José said

And abruptly, I couldn't help myself, I started laughing.

O'Larsen stared across at me, startled. Even José looked puzzled. I looked to him. "This is where we started," I said. "With a lawyer who didn't want the job and the whole thing being decided for us with no one caring at all, just everyone going through the motions."

José got it immediately. He smiled with recognition.

I grinned at him. "Wanna marry me again?"

And now he laughed. And even though they didn't know why we were laughing, the men on the benches behind us started laughing too. In a minute, all of us were laughing, mostly at

O'Larsen's puzzlement.

José turned to O'Larsen, started to speak, but I put a hand on his arm. "My turn." I looked through the glass at our unwilling representative. "Listen, here's the deal. Whether you or Yoh or anybody in charge recognizes it, José Rodríguez-Chan and myself, James Patrick Dolan, we are the authorized representatives of the Line Authority. We were duly sworn in and if you or whoever wants to send downline for confirmation, please do so. We are authorized to investigate, negotiate, and even sign treaties to guarantee the resumption of traffic on the Line. Failing that . . . well, we're also authorized to signal a complete closure of the portal, up to and including disengagement. Oh, and one more thing, we didn't lie. If downline doesn't hear from us on a regular schedule, they will take unilateral action—exactly as we told Coordinator Yoh. I assume he's already monitoring these discussions, but you can tell him that you looked through this glass barrier, looked into my eyes, saw the determination on my face, and realized that whatever else you might think we are—José and I can either be very good friends or very bad enemies. That's up to Coordinator Yoh or whoever to decide. But you'd better decide quickly, because I can tell you that my superior officers downline are going to become very frustrated and very impatient very shortly—a lot more frustrated and impatient than we are here. So when I say you all, and I mean you *all*—" I waved at his side of the room, but I meant the entire Praxis colony. "Whatever you think you want to do, you'd better come to the negotiating table very quickly. Or there won't be any negotiations. You have . . ." I glanced at my watch, ". . . maybe an hour."

O'Larsen kept his face immobile. I had to give him credit for that. It's probably something lawyers have to learn quickly, how to suppress their feelings. I don't know, I try not to have much contact with lawyers. Once was enough.

"I'll get back to you," he said.

"Wait. One more thing."

"What?"

"We will not negotiate anything unless we are respected as equals. Praxis colony will supply amenities to us and to—" I pointed to the men on the benches, "—all of the others who are accused. That includes beds, chairs, showers, food, and anything else that Coordinator Yoh and his team will have."

O'Larsen nodded. "I can't guarantee that."

"Then don't come back until you can."

Maybe his expression tightened, I couldn't tell. He turned stiffly and walked out.

José looked to me. "Wow. That was impressive." I barely heard him. The men behind us were applauding.

THIRTY-TWO

T o their credit, they didn't take long.

Less than thirty minutes later, a team of six men in gray bio-suits came in through the airlock, ferrying two conference tables, three carts with warm food, two with cold, another cart with drinks, padded chairs, and most of the artwork that had been stripped from the walls. Even the rugs were replaced.

This had been a proper conference room before it had been turned into a holding cell, and now it was being returned to its former appearance. The benches were quietly removed.

After they filed out, Anjin and Morne took charge of the room, sorting out duties and meals. When they signaled they were ready, all of us took our places at the tables and waited politely while one of them said grace, a very heartfelt gratitude for the moment.

The meal was simple, but it represented respect. Coffee, muffins, omelets, toast, butter, a variety of fruit and juice. We ate mostly in silence.

It didn't have to be said aloud. We had to demonstrate discipline so we could negotiate from credibility. We limited our chatter and did not discuss anything more important than, "Pass the salt, please."

After we finished our meal, the men of the team cleared the tables, disposed of the trash, returned the food containers to the carts, and rolled the carts to the back of the room. Anjin and Morne put their heads together and came to a quick agreement. Because José and I had the credentials, we would speak for the group.

And then we waited.

It didn't take long.

While we had been eating, a team on the other side of the glass had installed a proper conference table, chairs, and a flag of Praxis.

José and I exchanged a glance. "Damn, I knew we forgot something."

I shook my head and took out my phone, set it to projection mode, and put the flag of the Line Authority on our back wall. "Okay, now we're ready."

Coordinator Yoh and at least a dozen assistants entered the room on the other side of the glass. O'Larsen was not one of them. A good sign. We had been upgraded from prisoners to negotiators.

We all took our places at our respective tables, facing each other through the glass partition.

Coordinator Yoh arranged some things on the table before him. A pad of paper, a pen, a pitcher of water, some glasses. Finally, he looked up. "I am ready to hear what you have to say."

"We're not ready yet." I pointed to his water pitcher.

He looked annoyed, but he gestured to an assistant. The man spoke quietly into his phone.

A few moments later, the door at the back of the room slid open and a robot cart rolled in. A pitcher. Water. Glasses. One of the team members placed them in front of José and me.

"Now," I said. "I have something to say." I looked around the table for nods of assent. "For the past three Praxis days, if I have calculated the time correctly—for the past three Praxis days, we have all been engaged in a game of 'Let's whip it out and see whose is longest.' I don't know about you, but I'm tired of stroking for length. Let's come . . . to terms."

"You have a unique way with words," said Yoh.

"I needed to get your attention."

"You have my attention."

"Good."

"For the record, I assume you're recording this, I am James Patrick Dolan and this is my husband, José Rodríguez-Chan. My husband and I are authorized to act as legal representatives of the Line Authority. We are also part of the emigration group that has been stalled at North Station. We have, all of us, been as well trained as possible for life on this planet. We do acknowledge that there is still a great deal for us to learn. We also acknowledge that this is not the welcome we expected. Clearly, the situation has changed. What happens next, for both sides, is that we have an honest exchange of information so that we can proceed to a workable solution."

Coordinator Yoh nodded. He cleared his throat. He looked around his table as if to show that he had their full support. He turned back to us with a scowl. "I am Coordinator Yoh of the Praxis Authority."

He paused to refer to his notes. He looked at us again, this time his irritation was clear. "You claim to speak as friends or allies, but you have not behaved as such. You sent assault teams through the portal. That is an invasion. An act of war. Why should we trust you?"

"Why should we trust *you*?" I replied. "You closed the portal to all traffic without explanation."

"We had a situation."

"Obviously." I folded my hands in front of me and waited. José echoed my posture.

After a moment, the rest of the team did as well. I could have kissed them all.

THIRTY-THREE

Coordinator Yoh was not a happy man.

Back on Earth, we had spent several sessions in the training room reviewing the governance of Praxis, the laws and regulations, the agreements and the rules necessary not only for survival, but for acceptance as well. Yoh's name had come up a lot, but he had never been identified as a high-ranking official.

One of the portfolios described him as "an essentially unhappy man." But this was further acknowledged because, "he doesn't see things as they are. He sees them as he wants them to be." To the best of our knowledge back on Earth, he was a curdled idealist.

Now, sitting across from him, we could see that he had also become a cynical pragmatist. Whatever he needed to do to keep on keeping on— he would do it.

He met my gaze with undisturbed indifference, but he said nothing.

A useful tactic at any negotiating table. Sit

quietly. Say nothing. Force the other side to break the silence. The waiting game is another way to establish the power dynamic.

There is a way to break it, but it requires props. Take out a deck of cards, play solitaire. Or start a game of chess with the person next to you. Anything that indicates you are prepared to wait as long as necessary for the other side to respond.

But we didn't have the time.

I cleared my throat.

Yoh looked up.

"According to the records we had back on Earth, you were a minor functionary in the Praxis Authority. Let's see if I remember correctly." I paused for effect. "Um, Deputy Assistant in Charge of Breakfast? Something like that?"

That got to him.

"Senior Deputy, Economic Division. Imports and Exports."

"Ah, yes. Breakfast. And Lunch."

"You are trying to annoy me," he said.

"I'm not trying at all. I'm succeeding." And that gave me the conversational leverage I needed. I said, "We're waiting for you to explain what happened here on Praxis." And then I busied myself pouring water into glasses for myself and José and then the others at the table. "Would you like some water?" I asked each one. We passed glasses up and down the ranks. Finally I looked back to Yoh. "Whenever you're ready?"

Yoh looked at his aides and assistants.

He sighed in resignation. His shoulders sagged. Finally. He looked up again.

"There was an attempted coup," he said. "It was brutal. They murdered half the governing council. But some of us were late to that meeting. If we'd been there, you wouldn't be here now. We don't have a real military here, but we were able to effect an effective counter-effort. The details are . . . unnecessary. There are things we don't publicize. The council was aware of the possibility and had made some preparations. Maybe not as much as they should have, but ultimately we were successful. Some of the coup leaders escaped. We're still hunting them down. The ones we captured . . ." He stopped himself. "I wish we hadn't had to . . ." He waved it away, as if the memory was so unpleasant, he didn't even want to say the words.

He recomposed himself. "So . . . when your pod came through the portal and we detected your assault teams, we justifiably suspected a counterattack by coup sympathizers."

"Uh-huh, yes." I took a breath. I scratched my ear. I leaned back in my chair. "I just have one question."

"Yes?"

"How do we know that you, and all those people around you, are not the coup?"

Yoh looked across the table at me. "And how do we know that you are not another part of the coup? It's the same question."

THIRTY-FOUR

"The question before us," Yoh said, "is proof. Evidence. Verification."

"On both sides."

"Of course."

"All right. You tell us what you require from us and we'll tell you what we require from you."

Yoh nodded. He gestured to an assistant and the entire glass wall went blank.

José touched my arm. "You did good," he said.

"You think so?"

"It's progress."

"We're still prisoners."

"We have something they need. And they have something we need. That's where the deal-making starts. And in case I haven't told you before, you're a good negotiator."

I shrugged. "It's a personal skill. I learned it the hard way."

He squeezed my hand. "I've known that about you for a long time. You keep your strengths hidden until you have to use them."

I looked up, a suggestion that I was speaking for the hidden microphones. "We still have a few moves left. I hope we don't have to use them."

José glanced up, the quickest flick of his eyes, then back to me. He smiled.

"So . . ." I turned to the other men at the table. "This might get a little sticky. Can we count on you? Do we have your support?"

Anjin rose, Morne right behind him. "You stood up for us back on Earth when it was necessary, so I think I can speak for the rest of us now—" He looked around the room for disagreement. There was none. "Go ahead, Dolan. Do what you gotta do."

"Thank you. I appreciate that. Thank you." I wanted to say more, but decided not to. I took José off to a corner of the room and the two of us sat down facing each other. I needed to think. Again, I pointed toward the ceiling. He nodded.

"So what next?"

I pointed to the ceiling again. "We need to know who the good guys are. We need to talk to someone who can answer that question. We're working in the dark. We don't know what happened here, what the issues are. It could be about whether to break their eggs at the small end or the large—"

"I didn't realize you were that literate."

"I spent a lot of time hiding out in the library, remember? What about you?"

"I saw the movie."

"Which one?"

"The good one."

"There were several."

He waved it away. "Never mind. We'll argue about it later. You were saying—?"

"I was saying, we don't know what side we're on."

"I think we're on the side of the Line Authority."

"Well, yes—but what if the Line Authority has been, I dunno, wrong in all this?"

"As far as we know, the Line Authority is about keeping the Line open."

I nodded agreement. "But—"

"Uh-oh, you're going into lecture mode, aren't you?"

"Yes. And stop making faces. We have time."

"I'm not making faces."

"Tell that to your face."

"Okay, go ahead. I'm listening."

I took a breath. "Here's what I know. Back on Luna and Mars, I picked up some pamphlets."

"Printed pamphlets? People still do that?"

"A truly free press is impossible to monitor. Paper is cheap, but ideas are valuable."

"Who said that?"

"I just did."

"All right, all right, go on."

"Okay, just this. What I read is that the Line Authority is an Inter-World agency."

"Yes, I know that."

"To pay its bills, it levies a tax on all traffic. The profitable worlds pay a tax for every portal their cargo has to come through. Fair enough. The transfer stations have to be subsidized because they don't produce anything. But if there's a tax on every portal, then far enough out, no world could ever be profitable. So that sets an economic limit on how far the traffic can spread—the Line can't go past the place where the tax burden surpasses revenue. The colony just goes deeper into debt. And . . . we have enough history to demonstrate it, debt can be profitable. Not to the debtor, though."

José didn't say anything to that. He was thinking about our long-ago student loans. And all of the other costs of living on Earth. Pollution tax. Water tax. Security tax. A person had to earn three plastic dollars for every one he spent. And the minimum wage still hadn't caught up to the living wage. That's why Praxis looked like the great escape.

José looked across at me. "I think I see what you're getting at. We don't know what the problem is, do we?"

"That's what we have to find out. Then we'll know what to do. It's this simple. If you want to solve a problem, don't look at who's suffering from it, look at who's profiting from it."

THIRTY-FIVE

I continued. "And the second part of that problem..."

"The first part wasn't bad enough?"

I ignored the interruption. I did that sometimes. "The second part of that problem is that we don't know who to ask for guidance. Because everybody, and I mean everybody we know, everybody has their own agenda. We've been given the authority to decide the future of a whole world. And we have no one to depend on. We are on our own."

"Oh," said José. "Crap."

"Yeah. You said a mouthful."

"Ugh."

Silence, while he thought about what I'd said. The problem. Not the mouthful. "Okay, how do you want to proceed?"

"I don't know. All of my ideas are . . . impractical. How about you?"

He shook his head. "I got nothing. My best idea was marrying you."

"And you see how well that worked out."

He punched my arm. Not hard. But hard enough. "Don't ever say that again."

"It was a joke."

"It wasn't funny."

"Sorry."

"Apology accepted."

"Meanwhile . . . ?"

José sighed. "If all your ideas are impractical, then maybe just go for the one that's the least impractical . . . ?"

"There aren't any." I took his hands. "The thing is . . . whatever we do, it could blow up in our faces. We could end up making things worse than ever."

He pulled away, thinking. "Okay. As I see it, we have to prove they can trust us."

"Uh-huh. And they have to do the same. Prove that we can trust them."

"So, what do we do? What can we do?"

"And what can they do . . . ?"

"I see the problem," he said.

"And what if we discover we can't trust them?" I said.

"Yeah. Stalemate."

"Worst possible case? We close the line and go back down."

"Then what? The Labor Corps?"

"Maybe another planet."

"Another training? Oh, god no." He meant it as a joke. Mostly.

"Hey. Maybe we could be trainers. At least we'd eat regular."

"Being in the training room forever? You really want that?"

I didn't have to think about it. "All that endless drama? Oh, hell no." I took his hands again. "So I guess we have to make this one work. Don't we?"

He nodded. After a bit, he said, "I was thinking about something someone said once. Go big or go home. Maybe that's what we should do."

"Go big or go home. That's the opposite of what's the least impractical. But . . . it kinda makes sense. Especially here." I scratched my ear, thinking. "Maybe . . ."

"What?"

"What's the biggest thing we can do? The *most* impractical?"

He frowned. Then he got it. He looked at me. "That?"

"Yes, that."

THIRTY-SIX

I stopped myself. I looked at him. "José—" I said.

"What?"

"Reassure me?"

"What?!"

"You know me. I'm full of doubts. All the time."

'Yes, that's your strength. That's your intelligence at work. Stupid people never doubt themselves."

"Just, please. Reassure me."

"Okay, first of all, I married you because I recognized you were smart. Also adorable. But smart. And sometimes funny."

"I mean, about this plan."

"Oh, that? It's audacious. It probably won't work, nothing yet has worked the way it's supposed to, but this is the right thing to do."

"That's the best you can do? It probably won't work—"

"Yes." He met my gaze. "But it's the right thing to do."

I sighed. "You're right."

"Of course, I'm right. I'm smart enough to know when I'm right. Maybe someday you'll be that smart too."

"Oh, I'm that smart. I just like being reassured."

He punched my arm. Then he rubbed my shoulder. "You're something else."

"So are you. Let's do it."

We did.

THIRTY-SEVEN

I t took a while. There were a lot of pieces to put in place.

First, we sent our report down the line. We didn't know if they received it. We weren't getting any messages back. Coordinator Yoh must have shut down all the communication channels, including the power cables on which we were piggybacking our coded signals. I had to give him credit, he wasn't stupid. The real question was whether he was smart enough.

Or the Line Authority just wasn't responding, not even an acknowledgment that the message was received.

Next we sent out a coded signal to the assault teams that were still unrecovered. They didn't respond either, but they weren't supposed to.

We briefed Anjin and Morne what we were up to. They weren't happy with the plan, but they reluctantly agreed it might be our best chance.

And then, we waited.

We had lunch.

And dinner.

And napped.

And finally, at the most uncomfortable hour possible, an annoying sound buzzed us awake.

I rolled off the mattress that José and I shared and made my way to the front of the room, I rubbed the sleep from my eyes and stared through the glass, taking my time to assess what I was looking at. Behind me, other men were sitting up in their makeshift beds, wondering what was going on.

The glass wall was clear again and on the other side, a disheveled looking Coordinator Yoh, stood, surrounded by several of his aides. They looked equally unkempt.

"What the hell are you doing?" he demanded.

"Well, I was sleeping with my husband. Until you woke us."

José came up beside me. "You want coffee?" he asked. I nodded. He went off to one of the food carts.

Yoh composed himself. "You have sent a message to the Line Authority asking them to close the portal until further notice, and to ignore all messages from anyone claiming to be the government of Praxis. You sent it in the clear so that everyone would be able to read it—"

He opened his mouth to say more, but I held up a hand to stop him. To his credit, he stopped.

"First of all, I'm tired," I said. "I'm tired of you. I'm tired of the games you're playing. I'm tired of this room. I'm tired of this food. And I'm tired of Praxis and I don't care if we stay or go. You have been as useful here as a burlap condom, and a lot less fun. But—" I held up a hand while I figured out what next to say. "But—we came here in good faith with a commitment to build a new world and we are not yet ready to give up and go back. So everything we have done, everything that we have decided to do, all of it is about making Praxis work. Whether you like it or not."

He glowered at me. Good. Anger is a sign that the other side is emotionally off balance.

I continued. "Are you ready to work with us or not?"

He glowered some more.

"As a sign of our good faith, I have sent out a signal to the remaining teams who came across with us, the ones you still have not intercepted. We have asked them to make themselves known to the nearest authorities and from there to proceed here, where they will join us in our . . ." I waved my hand around, ". . . in our very generous captivity. That will be our demonstration that we are prepared to negotiate in very good faith." I leaned forward, as far as I could. "Are you?"

"You aren't giving me—us—much of a choice. Without the portal, we can't survive."

"Um, actually you can. We ran the metrics back on Earth, and I double-checked them here."

José came up beside me with a mug of coffee and my tablet. I held up the tablet. "According to this, human survival on an isolated Praxis is possible. Just not very pleasant. You'll have to give up coffee, for starters. And the imported protein as well. But you'll still have potatoes. Well, we'll all have potatoes. We'll be stuck here with you too. So you won't be alone in the resulting hardship. We'll share it with you. So, are we going to be partners or . . . what?"

Yoh said something in a language I didn't recognize, but the intent was clear.

"I'm not sure I'm limber enough to do that. Can I have my husband do the necessary?"

The glass wall went blank again.

I turned to José. "Well, that went well, don't you think?"

THIRTY-EIGHT

I sipped at my coffee. It wasn't bad. José knew I liked it with two sugars.

José scratched his neck. "You definitely have their attention."

"We need more than his attention. We need his compliance. All of theirs." I pulled up a chair and plopped down into it. José pulled up another. We looked at each other. There wasn't anything to say.

I put my coffee cup down and put my head in my hands. "I hope this works."

"It will," said José. "All politics is acting. And you're a very good actor."

"You think so."

"You had me convinced."

I smiled at that. I looked up at him. "There aren't any carrots here. I had to hit him with the stick."

"It worked, didn't it?"

"Maybe. They could still . . . I don't know."

"Yes, they could. But that would be the

stupid thing to do."

"José," I said. "I love you very much. Don't ever doubt that. But sometimes both of us can be stupid—stupid enough to think that stupid people are capable of intelligent behavior. They're not. They're just not. Every time, and I mean every time that I have said that someone can't be that stupid, I've been wrong. They just say, 'challenge accepted' and do the stupid thing anyway. So I started preparing for the stupid things, and for the most part, I've kept out of trouble. Well, except for the riot that got us sent here."

"Well, yeah, but you got a husband out of it."

"So did you. But I think I got the better deal."

"You ever say that again, I'll have to slap the stupid out of you."

"Okay, I surrender."

"It's late. Or maybe it's early. Do you want to go back to bed?"

"Yeah, I think so. They have a lot of arguing to do. It'll be a while before they come back to the table."

José took me by the hand and led me back the mattress we used as a bed. We curled up together and tried to fall asleep. But I couldn't. I ended up on my back, staring at the ceiling, trying not to imagine all the things that could still go wrong. Everything depended on Yoh. Did he want to be right or righteous?

THIRTY-NINE

We did not get an answer to that question for a full Praxis day.

We could only imagine the arguments.

We had a few ourselves.

Kovacs and the rest of the assault teams were ushered into the room. It was getting crowded in here. The men greeted each other warmly, some with hugs and kisses. It took a while for everyone to calm down.

But Kovacs came directly to me. "Okay, Dolan. What the hell are you doing?"

I looked to José. "Haven't we already had this conversation?"

"I guess we have to have it again."

I looked to Kovacs. "Do you trust me?"

"No," he said. Then he reconsidered. "Okay, yes. But you'd better have a good explanation."

I pointed toward the ceiling. "I'm pretty sure we're being recorded. And I don't want to give them any more information than I have to."

Kovacs frowned. "Do you know what you're doing?"

"As much as any of us know what we're doing, yes. I think so."

Grudgingly, he accepted that. "What can you tell me?"

I showed him my credentials. "This. This is it. José and I are now the highest-ranking officials in the entire Praxis colony. We are the Line Authority. And what we say goes. So we can shut down the entire portal and isolate this world until they come to terms."

"Or they can have you murdered and negotiate from there."

"Yes, we considered that. And yes, they could, but I doubt the Line Authority would be amenable to any negotiations after that. But just in case, we closed the portal until José or myself reopens it."

Kovacs looked around the large room, the tables, chairs, mattresses, the food trollies. "Well, this looks a lot better than camping out in the wind. How's the food?"

"Not bad. Help yourselves. The quality of the accommodations suggests they don't know yet what to do with us. Honor us or kill us. So that's a good sign."

I grabbed Kovacs and hugged him like a long-lost friend. I whispered into his ear, "Don't read anything into this," I whispered. "If they're watching . . ."

"Right." He nodded against me. "Just so you'll know. We stashed our weapons before we surrendered ourselves. I doubt they'll find them."

I whispered back, "That's good. But don't tell me where. Don't tell me anything I don't need to know."

"Right."

We broke apart and I realized José was giving me a jealous stare. But he meant it in jest and quickly smiled. He understood.

Our captors left the transport pod connected through a set of airlocks and most of the men on the assault teams moved into it. The bus had a bigger shower, cabins, better beds, and a mostly full larder. José and I, Kovacs, Anjin and Morne, stayed in the conference room to be ready for any further negotiations.

There is this about Praxis. Most of the structures are converted pods. Because the pods all have airlocks, visitors in bio-suits can go out on the surface and return to specifically assigned shelters. They can also, under certain circumstances mingle with permanent residents. But while this allowed some interaction, it was also a serious limit. There were places we could not go and therefore, people we could not meet.

The five of us exchanged notes on a well-shielded pad of paper. Paper was one of the major exports of Praxis, produced by drying, shredding, pulping, treating, and drying a particularly sludgy kind of noxious seaweed that otherwise would have clogged up waterworks. But it was good paper and apparently much in demand downline.

As much as we wanted to speed things up by talking, we had to keep our conversation to a minimum. We traded furious notes back and forth between us, afterward shredding each sheet and dropping it into a waste bucket.

I presented my ideas. José added his suggestions. Anjin expressed his doubts. Morne was against it. Kovacs was willing to be convinced. We started from there and the conversation went back and forth for several hours, with occasional breaks for coffee and sandwiches—or to ask for more pads. Eventually we developed a kind of shorthand, using convenient acronyms and abbreviations. We took the plan apart and put it back together again, but in the end, we had a consensus.

Now all we had to do was wait.

FORTY

The glass wall cleared.

Yoh sat quietly on the other side of the table. He was alone.

We took our places at our table, facing him. We looked at each other, everyone nodded. I was still the primary spokesman.

"For the record," he began. "We do not monitor your conversations in the pods, nor in the conference room. We do not listen, we do not record, we do not intercept your coded communications. We do not look over your shoulders as you write your separate notes. To do so would be unethical. We are not evil men."

I looked to the others, I looked back to him. "We appreciate your assurance. But we will continue to take precautions."

"As you will." He poured himself a glass of water, drank slowly. He put it down and looked at me. "Now, let's get to business. What do you want?" He spoke calmly.

"We want full access," I said.

"That's not possible," said Yoh. "There are places where your bio-suits can't go."

Again I exchanged glances with my team. They all nodded. I cleared my throat. "We came here as immigrants. All of us. We are ready to leave the protection of our bio-suits."

Yoh shook his head. "That eliminates any possibility of sending you back. We would be stuck with you."

"Yes," I agreed. "That is correct."

Across the table, Coordinator Yoh frowned, just the slightest expression of disapproval. I looked to Kovacs. He gave me a slight shrug. I looked to José. He nodded.

Yoh was still thinking it over. Finally, he said, "You five. No one else."

I wanted to relax in my seat, but not yet. This was a major concession on his part, but there were dangers too.

"May we confer?"

Yoh nodded. The glass wall went blank.

We pulled our chairs into a circle. "Can we trust him not to listen?" Morne asked. "I wouldn't trust my own grandmother in a place like this," Kovacs said.

I held up a hand, they fell silent. "Let's assume nothing. But I think at this point, we can talk candidly among ourselves. Only us five? No one else? That's a step in the right direction, but it's still a limit."

"It's dangerous," said Kovacs. "It gives them

the opportunity to isolate and maybe remove the leadership of this . . . delegation." That was one of our decisions. We were no longer an assault team. We were a delegation.

"We all have deputies," said Morne. "The delegation wouldn't be leaderless."

Anjin said, "And if they had to choose new leaders, they could. They know how to organize. They wouldn't be leaderless for long."

"If we accept their offer, it would be a sign of trust."

"We haven't trusted them so far."

"They haven't trusted us."

"Nobody trusts anybody. That's how life works."

"I'm beginning to understand why human history is such a mess," José said.

I grinned at him. "What took you so long?"

"*Mi abuela.* My grandmother. She always said, *'Sin confianza no puede haber amor.'* Without trust, there can be no love."

"Wow." I clutched my chest in mock agony. "Straight to the heart."

Kovacs interrupted. "Let's stick to the subject. Do we accept or not?"

Anjin raised his hand. "Let's make a counteroffer. Ten men. Five teams of two. Five independent investigations. We meet again here in three Praxis days."

"They'll give us one."

"One day is enough. Let's ask for three. Give

him something to counteroffer so he can claim a victory of his own."

I looked around. "Does anyone think we can do better? Do we want to try for more?"

We considered a few more ideas and discarded them just as quickly. This was progress.

"All right," I said. "Back to the table."

We resumed our places and waited for Yoh to clear the glass.

FORTY-ONE

T hree teams. Two men each.

José and I were one team. Anjin chose one of his men, they were the second team. Morne chose one of his, they were the third. Kovacs stayed behind.

We went through a separate series of airlocks into a changing room. We stopped, we hesitated. I looked to José. "This is it," I said.

He nodded agreement and began to unzip his bio-suit.

I did too.

The others also.

We dropped the suits into a hamper.

We stepped into the showers and scrubbed in three different sprays and finally a long and very thorough rinse cycle.

We stepped out into the drying room where we found plain white jumpsuits, apparently the standard uniform for new residents of Praxis.

Each team had two guides assigned to us, but they were not allowed to prevent us from visiting any part of any settlement unless it was specifically dangerous to residents or ourselves. Anjin's team went to the farms. He grew up in Iowa, he believed that Praxis' farmers would have the clearest sense of the situation.

Morne was the son of two teachers. He wanted to visit the University. Praxis had created its first schools long before any babies were started in the colony's industrial wombs. The first settlers had declared a mission statement, and among their assertions, they said that education was a lifelong journey. It had to be, especially on a new world.

José and I, we decided to take a walk along 6.5B Broadway, the main street of Dersham Station. Calling it Main Street was an understatement. It bordered both sides of a river at the bottom of a steep canyon, almost a klick cut into the surface.

Much of the surface of Praxis is badly fractured. If you get off the plains of the southern hemisphere, there are some astonishingly steep canyons, many of them steeper than Dersham. A few have been roofed over and inhabited, with dwellings up and down the sides. Shops and stores and services are mostly on the floor of the canyon, but also on wide platforms carved into the red-brown rock. Frequent elevators run up and down the walls.

The Praxologists love this part of Dersham because they have unlimited access to six and a half billion years of sedimentary layers. The history of the planet was on display here. There had been seas here, glaciers, earthquakes, volcanic eruptions, continental collisions, mountains, recessions, valleys, more seas, more quakes, more volcanoes, even a few asteroid collisions.

They still haven't finished cataloging all the layers, it's a lifetime job, but we learned quickly that it was a local joke. Addresses were calculated by how deep the stores or dwellings were dug into the past. The floor of the canyon was 6.5B. After that, the numbers were north-south or east-west where the canyon bent to the east.

We held hands unashamedly. Couples were a common sight here and after the initial surprise of this very different new place, we began to smile. Above us, the steep walls of the canyon were lit with banners and signs and displays and decorations of all kinds.

José pointed up. "It looks like it's a holiday."

A couple passing by heard him and stopped to explain. One of the men said, "It's Celebration Day."

"We're new here. What's Celebration Day?"

"It's a local holiday. Every station has its own celebration day—the anniversary of the station's founding. The idea is to celebrate what's wonderful in your life."

"Ah. What a marvelous idea. Thank you."

"You too. Have a great day."

José smiled and squeezed my hand. He said,

"I celebrate you. I celebrate us."

"Me too. You're the best thing that ever happened in my life."

"You too."

We laughed together. Then we hugged. And kissed. "Welcome to Praxis," he said.

After a moment, I pulled apart. Reluctantly. "We still have work to do."

"Yeah. I know. *Mi amor*."

"*Si*," I replied.

We found a sidewalk café and studied the menu. Someone in the kitchen was a very inventive chef. José pointed at a picture. "This looks good."

"What do they use for money here?"

"Line dollars, I think."

"We'll ask the waiter."

We turned our chairs to face the avenue and the river beyond. There were no private cars, only trollies and scooters and the occasional small delivery truck. Above, there were cable cars at various levels.

"There's too much to see."

José nodded. "The pictures are one thing. Being here—" He shook his head in amazement. "It's something else."

"You're new here, aren't you?" That was the waiter, a young man with bright blue hair.

"How can you tell?"

"It's the jumpsuits. Welcome to Praxis. Put your wallets away. Newbies get free drinks. It's a tradition. And it's Celebration day."

"What's the most popular drink on Praxis? We'll have two of those."

"Good choice. But let me suggest a Celebration Special. We only serve it today."

"Okay," I said. "Two of those."

The waiter disappeared somewhere inside, but he must have pointed us out to some of the other customers—or maybe our jumpsuits served as billboards. In a short time, our table was surrounded by cheerful men, eager to chat with us. Some single men, some couples, old, young, mostly happy and curious. Some sat for a while, some just long enough to say hello.

"What's the situation on Earth?"

"Did you spend any time on Luna or Mars?"

"Have they restored the portal?"

"We're working on that," José said.

"Are you part of the new immigration?"

"It's complicated, but yes," I said. "Apparently, there was some situation, I think it's being resolved. What happened on this side?"

"The same old same old."

Our drinks arrived then and we discovered they were . . . interesting. A little bit sweet and a little bit sparkly, but some very distinct fruity flavor we couldn't identify.

The conversation wandered randomly from subject to subject—the weather on the east, the construction of the new farms, the feasibility of an orbital elevator, the new club opening at the north end of the canyon, whether or not older men should wear shorts or skirts, who was the better actor in the touring company of *A Martian Story*, and if the Symphony's new conductor was better with Tchaikovsky or Saint-Saens.

We let the conversation wander. It gave us a good sense that most of the men here on Praxis were enjoying their lives. But occasionally, José or I would ask a question that might allow a political observation. The answers came back as vague as the questions.

After a while, someone suggested dinner, and a group of us adjourned to a nearby restaurant, also overlooking the river. A team of young shirtless men came rowing by, practicing for an upcoming competition.

"Nice view," remarked José.

"They're a good team," said one of our hosts, "but probably not a match for the fellows from Eastern. They won't admit it, but we're pretty sure they're modifying."

Dinner was delicious, thin slabs of cultured meat lurking under some kind of yellow sauce. The names were in French so we weren't sure what we were eating, but it was good, and the desserts were amazing. Something called *crepes*.

Our hosts tried quizzing us, we answered some of their questions accurately, especially the trainings. They compared their own experiences and remarked on how the trainings for Praxis had changed since their time. We did not say much about our current circumstances.

Finally, though, I began to suspect that perhaps some of our hosts had been sent to us by Coordinator Yoh. It wasn't impossible for him to have set that up. So I came right out and said it. "We heard there was . . . a coup, or an attempted coup, or something. Some kind of political thing? Can you tell us anything about that?"

José glanced at me meaningfully, but said nothing. If they were Coordinator Yoh's men, their answers would tell us that. Several of the men looked at each other, perhaps wondering if they should say anything. But one of them shrugged and said, "Look, as long as there's food on the table, nobody's going to complain. That's been the Praxis way of life for . . . I dunno, maybe since we started."

Another one shook his head. "That's one way of thinking yes. We do our jobs, we keep out of trouble. We make sure that everybody survives."

"And there's another way of thinking?"

"The next step. We try to make tomorrow better than yesterday. Some of us want to start families. That means we have to be more than self-sufficient, we have to be able to grow. So . . . yeah, there's some politics involved. But most of us," he looked to the first speaker, "we come at it from different sides, but most of us are agreed on the long-term goals."

'But what about the . . . was it a coup? Or what?"

"It was a bunch of spoiled brats wanting to

get their way."

Another one of the men spoke up then. "Maybe some people who never should have been allowed to immigrate. How they got through the training—?"

And a third. "Both sides—instead of finding ways to work together, they were looking for ways to punish each other." He shook his head in disgust.

"So, who won? The good guys or the bad guys?"

"Nobody won," said a gray-haired man who had been sitting quietly at the far end of the table. "Nobody won. There were no good guys. There were no bad guys. We all lost. All that time and energy—wasted."

Nobody replied to that. This man was respected here.

"I'm sorry, sir. I didn't catch your name."

"Benjamin Hodel."

"Hodel?" I gasped. "The philosopher? I read your book!"

"Thank you. I wonder if you were the only one."

"Everybody read it."

"That must have been after I left—"

"The right to celebrate. It was one of the reasons for the riot—"

"Then you didn't read it at all."

I shut up. He was right.

FORTY-TWO

José broke the silence. He said, "Most of our dealings were with . . . Coordinator Yoh. He's an odd bird, isn't he? We couldn't figure him out."

Somebody snorted. "Yoh? He's an asshole. But he follows the Covenant."

"He's not gonna survive the next election."

"Nah, he's gonna win a mandate."

"We've had worse."

"Yeah, but we want better."

"Then why don't you stand for office."

"Hell, no. I might get elected."

Some laughter at that. The conversation continued in that vein for a while, we had coffee and after-dinner chocolates (imported), and when the evening lights came on, illuminating the high walls of the canyon like shimmering curtains, José and I thanked our hosts and excused ourselves.

We walked along the banks of the river, under the massive trees studded with thousands of shimmering lights. We admired the gardens and the flowers and the frequent art installations. "This is a very rich world," said José.

"This part is. The rest, we don't know. I think the people we met might be isolated from the harsher parts of Praxian life."

"Maybe." He stopped me at a wide spot overlooking a place where the water splashed over shallow rocks. He reached over and held my hand. "You're de facto leader of this whole thing."

"I didn't want to be."

"But you are."

"I don't know what to do."

"You'll do what you always do. You'll find a way to make it right."

"Nothing's right here." I took both his hands in mine. I looked at him for a long moment, studying his shining eyes, the sweetness of his expression. "Okay, look—" I led him over to a bench where we could sit and watch the river. "This is who I am, José—a performance of who I think I have to be. And the only time I'm not a performance is at night, in bed, when you and I just holding each other. That's when I'm finally me. I surrender—I surrender to you. Nobody else."

I sniffled. I hadn't realized this would be so hard to say.

"All my life. The people around me, all I ever see in them is their performance—who they want the rest of us to see and believe. It's like everybody's a phony, a fraud, all trying to live up to some ideal that nobody really believes in."

I took his hands in mine again. "I'm tired of being a fraud. I want to . . . I want to tell people I'm annoyed and frustrated and cranky and pissed off and furious with the whole damn thing, everything. I want everybody around me to stop being assholes and start being real. Authentic. And the thing is . . ." I almost laughed. "I'm not even sure we're authentic. You and I. Except somehow, sometimes, like at night mostly, I know we can be. And that has to be enough. Because even if that's all there is, it's a lot more than nothing."

He nodded thoughtfully. "Maybe it's because at night we're too tired to put on the performance . . . ?"

I had to laugh at that. "You're right."

José held my hands, now it was his turn. "You are a remarkable man, James Patrick Dolan. You are much more than I ever imagined you would be. And I cherish you for that—"

"I'm only remarkable because of you—"

"Don't make me slap you again—"

"Sorry."

"—I trust you to find a way to find a way to say it. A way that works for all of us. Because I know you. You'll go silent. You'll withdraw from everything and you'll worry about it so hard that your eyes will turn red and smoke will come out of your ears and the gears in your head will make the most amazing grinding noises, but when all of that is done, you'll have something important to say. And everybody will stop and listen."

I didn't know what to say to that. So I said nothing.

I hoped he was right. I had to trust him.

We sat in silence and watched the river. Reflections of the evening lights glittered in the water.

After a while, José put his head on my shoulder.

I felt nice.

FORTY-THREE

This time, we were on Yoh's side of the conference room. It felt weird looking at our colleagues, our teammates with a wall between us. The men on the other side of the glass were eager to hear what we had learned.

The six of us, José and myself, Anjin and Morne and their two teammates, sat around the conference table and compared notes. It wasn't a complete picture, it was mostly anecdata. But it gave us an interesting perspective.

What all of us had found was that some of the citizens of Praxis absolutely did not care who was running their government as long as they were left alone to do their jobs. Others had very strong opinions, but rarely spoke them because they didn't like getting into arguments. And a third group had a low opinion of just about everything, but especially authority of any kind. That's why they had immigrated. There were also a few who just came for the parties, but that was understandable too. Praxis was always seen as an escape.

After two hours of listening, a lot of coffee, some kind of pickles and crackers, two pee breaks, a sandwich, more coffee, and a suppressed urge to hit something, I wrote an observation on the pad of paper in front of me. "Arrogance and ignorance all in one place. How convenient."

I showed it to José and he nodded.

He scrawled back. "Who are you talking about?"

I wrote. "Everybody." And shoved it back at him. After a moment, I pulled it back and added, "Me too."

He looked at it, thought about it, nodded, and smiled.

I stood up. "Okay, I think we've established that there is nothing else to establish. Let's talk to Coordinator Yoh."

Kovacs agreed. The others sat back in their chairs, exhausted. They had nothing to say either. Kovacs stood up, went to a wall panel and pressed the white button with his thumb. "We're ready," he said.

Eventually, Yoh and several aides came in. They sat at the opposite end of the table, facing us, visibly hostile.

For the first hour, there was the usual posturing, the usual performances of welcome and hope and cooperation. The usual bullshit. We said what we had to. They said what they had to. We repeated ourselves. They repeated themselves.

Halfway through the second hour of this, we took a half-hour break.

I got up and went to take a long shower. José joined me for a while and rubbed my back. Try as he could, he could not get the tension out of my shoulders.

"Jamie," he said. "You're in charge here. It's time to stop listening and start doing what you do best. Lead."

I didn't like it, but he was right.

I went back into the room. I watched them gather, resuming their previous places around the big conference table.

But I didn't sit down.

I stood apart and pointed at the table. "This is the part of the problem. Coordinator Yoh, you and your people are sitting at one end of the table, we're sitting at the other. Look at the context. That's an adversarial position. That's why we're not getting anything done here. We're just playing our performances for each other."

Coordinator Yoh didn't speak. He waited. That was his tactic. Sit and wait for the other side to speak. Because when the other side speaks first, it's a moment of surrender. He's giving away some of his power. Yoh was very good at sitting and waiting.

But I was better at talking. That's what José said, anyway.

"If we're going to get anything useful done in here, then we've gotta stop being adversaries.

We're all people of Praxis now. We have to find ways to communicate and cooperate together. Or we'll never get anywhere. So here, let's try this. Alternate sitting. One of yours, one of ours. Yeah, like that. Now pass the donuts around."

FORTY-FOUR

I didn't think it would work, but I was desperate enough to try.

And for a while, everybody was uncomfortable with this new seating arrangement. Nothing useful was said by anybody. We went around the table three times, each time reviewing and repeating all the previous assertions.

But then one of Yoh's aides, probably not knowing that he should have kept his mouth shut, raised a question about the costs of the Line and Anjin's assistant across from him promptly answered with some facts about portal taxes, and that opened up the discussion for others on both sides to add their own complaints about the economics of the Line and in a few moments everyone was complaining about the same things, and finally there was some agreement in the room about something.

The discussion got a little heated then, but the target of the anger was the Line, not each other, and José and I exchanged a glance that suggested maybe something was happening here.

There was a lot we didn't know about Praxis and the Praxians were justifiably annoyed that the immigrants arrived with false hopes and expectations, but they understood that wasn't the fault of the immigrants, it was the failure of the training agencies and the Line Authority. Identifying those problems opened up the discussion to identify some of the bigger problems, the underlying ones, the economic ones. A few solutions were considered, none of them immediately workable, but both sides were finally having a pragmatic discussion about how some challenges could be addressed. On both sides.

I listened. José and Kovacs made notes. So did several of Yoh's team. The Coordinator, however, said nothing. I sat opposite him and watched him carefully. He studied me too. I smiled. He didn't. He sat back in his chair, his arms folded across his chest, listening but scowling.

Eventually he shook his head. He rose and walked from the room without saying a word.

His aides got up and followed.

I looked to the others. "I think the answer is no."

Except—

The last aide out the door turned and looked back at us. He held up a hand to indicate "Wait."

The door closed behind him.

José looked to me. "What was that?"

"I don't know."

FORTY-FIVE

They sent a note. "Wait. We'll let you know when we can resume."

"That's some very odd phrasing," José said.

Kovacs scratched his head. "Something's up."

"Yeah," I agreed. "Right. Let's take a break. Shower. Shit. Eat. Nap. Or vice versa, I don't care. But take care of the body, so the body can take care of the mind. Isn't that what they said in the training? Let's get some rest and then we'll reflect."

We had a few hours, not many, but enough. When they were ready to resume, they came back without Yoh.

"Where's the Coordinator?" I asked.

"He retired. I'm the Acting Coordinator now," said the senior aide. He identified himself as Qattar Singh. "You may regard me as the senior-most representative of the Praxis Station Authority."

"May we ask. Did he retire? Or was he . . . um,

replaced?"

"Does it matter? We have work to do." Singh pointed his assistants around the table, again in the alternate seating arrangement. He settled himself in the chair that Yoh had previously warmed.

After he was settled, Singh opened a portfolio in front of him. "Before we start, let me explain something. Your group, all hundred and thirty of you, you are the second largest immigration in the history of Praxis. We've reviewed your folders and we expect you to be valuable addition to the station. You all have a lot of useful and necessary skills. Indeed, our local orchestra will especially welcome the violin and saxophone players. But—" he paused. "The last big immigration created a lot of problems. Assimilation wasn't as easy as we'd hoped. So there was some resistance here, considerable resistance, by some elements who were afraid that the Line Authority was dumping another load of problems here. That's one of the reasons why the training you went through was drastically different than the previous courses. It couldn't just be about living on Praxis, it had to be about the kind of people we were getting, and . . ." he trailed off for a moment, perhaps remembering the past. He looked into his portfolio, but the answer wasn't there either. He took a breath, looked around at us and continued candidly. "So you see, it isn't just the problems we've had here, it's also been the problem that all of you represent."

"Is that why Yoh was replaced?"

"You really need to know?"

"Yes. If we're going to be honest here, yes."

"Because he was an obstacle. You weren't going to get anywhere with him," Singh said. "Yoh wasn't respecting the established lines of authority. That way lies chaos. We tried chaos. It didn't work. Now we're ready to try something else."

He stopped. He took another deep breath. "There," he said. "It's all on the table. Where do we go from here?" He waited for my answer.

They all waited.

They were all looking at me. I do not like being looked at. I long ago realized that it was a predator stare, the intense look of a lion before it goes after the prey. But in humans, it's supposed to mean something else. I composed myself and looked around the table, meeting the gaze of everyone there.

"Why me?" I asked. "No, seriously. Why me?"

"Because," said Singh. "You're the appointed representative of the Line Authority. The way the covenants are written, you outrank us. You are the senior-most official on Praxis."

"Oh," I said.

José poked me in the ribs. "Told you."

EPILOGUE

There is a three-story display in Celebration Park, the largest display in any of the station's parks. It was erected thirteen years after the passing of Coordinator James Patrick Dolan, and with the approval of his husband, José Rodríguez-Chan.

Once an hour, the screen shows a much younger James Patrick Dolan delivering his most famous speech, now known as the Declaration of Interdependence.

Historians have shown that much of the speech was derived from earlier sources. Dolan was a complex man, well-educated, but self-doubting, given to long periods of personal brooding, punctuated by periods of extreme passion. While this speech represented his commitment to the betterment of Praxis, it also reveals a great deal about the man himself.

Here is the speech:

I am not here to make friends. I am here to sort out the mess that everyone else has made and nobody wants to clean up.

Here's the way it looks to me. You don't have to like it. I don't.

All sides are wrong.

Everyone is wrong.

Because everyone is pursuing their own agenda.

And if you think that you're right about anything, you're even more wrong. Because as near as I can tell, none of you are thinking about how to make it work for anyone else.

The Line Authority . . . well, maybe they mean well, I'm supposed to speak for them, but today I'm speaking for us. Their mission, as they present it, is the colonization of new worlds, expanding the reach of humanity. But the structure of that expansion is the same mistake Britain made in the 1700's. The wealth was going back to Britain, not much of it was staying in the colonies. Whole forests were stripped just to build a thousand ships for their fleets. Eventually, there was a rebellion. A necessary rebellion. Or not. You can all argue about that on your own time.

But the same situation exists here. The Line shows a profit. The outworlds don't.

And the coup or the reorganization or whatever you want to call it. There were people who were wrong for thinking that violence is an answer. It isn't. Sometimes it's a necessary evil, but history shows that most revolutions, no matter how well-intentioned, end up replacing one bad agenda with another. The American revolution—no matter what they tell you, it wasn't about liberty, it was about economics, and the nation they built was a history of mad scrabbling for wealth. The rest of the world too. That's where they failed. That's what destroyed them. We're still picking up the pieces, how many centuries later?

And the existing authority here on Praxis? You know it better than I. It existed solely to cooperate with the Line Authority. Their motto was the same as all the other enablers. Don't rock the damn boat. Not while we're showing a profit.

And finally, let me talk about the trainings back on Earth—that's another agency formed by and run by the Line Authority, with the cooperation of the authorities here at Praxis Station, specifically to provide more colonists to further strengthen the existing status quo.

And the status quo is always the enemy. Always.

Because the status quo is based on continuing the past. It isn't about building the future

Yeah, the truth is ugly. Deal with it. Or don't. But if you don't, you're stuck in the convenient lie.

I don't expect anyone to like this. The Line Authority won't. The trainers and the training company won't. The Praxis authority won't like it. Some of the local self-appointed revolutionaries, maybe, but probably not. They're assholes too.

And to be blunt, I don't even like it myself.

But here's what's what anyway.

You haven't given me the authority as much as you've abandoned your claim on it. And the Line Authority thinks they've given me the authority to solve their problem here as well, but no—no, to all of that. I am not here to solve their problem either.

I have been thrust into this position because the rest of you were so busy arguing among yourselves, you forgot what you were supposed to be committed to.

I really do not want this job. But now that I have it, I intend to do the best I can, even though I can't imagine anything less satisfying than managing a herd of squabbling spoiled brats.

And frankly, based on everything I've seen everywhere, if human beings are supposed to be the missing link between apes and sentient life, we're still much too close to the chimpanzee side of that journey.

So here's what we're going to do.

We're going to create a temporary protectorate to keep Praxis running while we decide the next steps. The protectorate will consist of a council of seven. The council will have two members representing the present government, two members of the dissident faction, and two members of our immigrant delegation. The presiding officer of that council will be chosen by unanimous consent of the other six members. They will have 72 hours to choose or I will take on the job of leadership until such time as a suitable replacement can be found, but not longer than one Praxis year, because I'm already exhausted by this crap.

The Praxis Council will have 18 months to write a constitution, or a covenant, or a set of agreements, call it what you will, followed by another six months of public discussion and any necessary revisions.

That Constitution must allow all citizens of Praxis a voice in whatever governing body is finally approved.

The approval of that Constitution will require a two-thirds majority of the entire population.

Oh, and Praxis needs a firm commitment to public education, especially adult education. A democratic republic requires an informed electorate. Anything less than that and you get a rerun of this mess.

We depend on each other. All of us. All the time. It's essential to a working economy, a working community, a working world. That's why we have to make sure that nobody is left out.

Nobody can be left out. Otherwise, everything falls apart. Again.

Just as an aside, it shouldn't be too hard. There are, at last count, over a hundred drafts of possible constitutions to start with, plus commentaries on what works and what doesn't work. Pick what works.

The goal here is to create a working government. A functioning entity that serves the best interests of the people who live here—the goal is to create the most good for the most people. The goal is to create a government that is of the people, by the people, for the people, and always accountable to the people.

And when that's done, then I can finally retire. I look forward to it.

And one more thing. The governing council will also have the authority to declare Praxis an independent state. We will not be the property of a corporation. We will not be the colony of an offshore government. We will declare our independence. If the Line Authority doesn't like it, they can close the portal—or they can negotiate a fair-trade treaty with us.

And no, I am not taking questions. Argue among yourselves all you want, but this is the way it's going to be because I'm sick and fucking tired of the whole lot of you.

You can now start fighting among yourselves—as long as necessary before you finally accept the inevitable.

You are a starfaring species. You are the product of three billion years of evolution. Fucking act like it.

Okay, I'm done.

ABOUT THE AUTHOR

David Gerrold's work is known around the world. His novels and stories have been translated into more than a dozen languages. His TV scripts are estimated to have been seen by more than a billion viewers.

Gerrold's prolific output includes stage shows, teleplays, film scripts, educational films, computer software, comic books, more than 50 novels and anthologies, and hundreds of articles, columns, and short stories.

He has worked on a dozen different TV series, including *Star Trek, Land of the Lost, Twilight Zone, Star Trek: The Next Generation, Babylon 5,* and *Sliders.* He is the author of *Star Trek*'s most popular episode "The Trouble With Tribbles."

Many of his novels are classics of the science fiction genre, including *The Man Who Folded Himself,* the ultimate time travel story, and *When HARLIE Was One,* considered one of the most thoughtful tales of artificial intelligence ever written. His stunning novels on ecological invasion, *A Matter For Men*, *A Day For Damnation*, *A Rage For Revenge*, and *A Season For Slaughter*, have all been best sellers with a devoted fan following. His young adult series, *The Dingilliad*, traces the healing journey of a troubled family from Earth to a far-flung colony on another world. His *Star Wolf* series of novels about the psychological nature of interstellar war are in development as a television series.

A ten-time Hugo and Nebula award nominee, David Gerrold is also a recipient of the Skylark Award for Excellence in Imaginative Fiction, the Bram Stoker Award for Superior Achievement in Horror, and the Forrest J. Ackerman lifetime achievement award.

In 1995, Gerrold shared the adventure of how he adopted his son in *The Martian Child*, a semi-autobiographical tale of a science fiction writer who adopts a little boy, only to discover he might be a Martian. *The Martian Child* won the science fiction triple crown: the Hugo, the Nebula, and the Locus. It was the basis for the 2007 film *Martian Child* starring John Cusack and Amanda Peet.

Gerrold's greatest writing strengths are generally acknowledged to be his readable prose, his easy wit, his facility with action, the accuracy of his science, and the passions of his characters. An accomplished lecturer and world traveler, he has made appearances all over the United States,

England, Europe, Canada, Australia, and New Zealand. His easy-going manner and disarming humor have made him a perennial favorite with audiences.

David Gerrold is the 2022 winner of the Robert A. Heinlein Award.

BOOKS BY THIS AUTHOR

Brought to you by Starship Sloane Publishing

Praxis ($12.99 print & $9.99 eBook)

The Man Without a Planet ($10.99 print & $8.99 eBook)

Here There Be Lawyers ($13.99 print & $9.99 eBook)

The Boy Who Was Girl ($12.99 print & $9.99 eBook)

The Girl Who Was Silver ($12.99 print & $9.99 eBook)

Available everywhere that great books are sold!

FORTHCOMING BOOKS BY THIS AUTHOR

The Praxis Papers (Praxis I & II)

Thank you for purchasing this book.

DAVID GERROLD

THE GIRL

WHO WAS

SILVER

|Danger on the Other Side|

FOREWORD BY AJ DALTON